John Vornholt has had several writing and performing careers, ranging from being a stuntman in the movies to writing animated cartoons. After spending fifteen years as a freelance journalist, John turned to book publishing in 1989. Since then, he has written and sold more than fifty books for both adults and children, including several *New York Times* bestsellers. John currently lives with his wife and children in Tucson, Arizona.

Please visit his web-site at www.vornholt.net and the Troll King web-site at www.troll-king.com

You can find out more about John Vornholt and other Atom authors by visiting www.atombooks.co.uk

By John Vornholt

The Troll King Trilogy
THE TROLL KING
THE TROLL QUEEN
THE TROLL TREASURE

THE TROLL
TREASURE

John Vornholt

Typeset in Cochin by
Palimpsest Book Production Limited,
Polmont, Stirlingshire
Printed and bound in Great Britain by
Bookmarque Ltd, Croydon, Surrey

Atom Books

www.atombooks.co.uk

An *Atom* Book

First published in Great Britain by Atom 2005

Copyright © 2003 by John Vornholt

The moral right of the author has been asserted.

A CIP catalogue record for this book is available from
the British Library.

ISBN 1 904233 59 7

For Brian and Frances

ONE

Start At The Bottom

The ground shook, and geysers spewed fountains of steam into the sooty air at the bottom of the Great Chasm. The gigantic toad, Old Belch, leaped clear across the river of lava and landed on the opposite bank, causing the ground to shake even more. The troll and his friends had just climbed off the monstrous toad, and none of them knew where the beast was headed.

Twisted, gnarled plants snapped at Rollo's feet, and the hulking troll stumbled to the ground. Trying to steady himself, he reached out for a black rock and burned his palm on the hot surface.

'Yow!' cried the troll who would be king, blowing the sparks off his singed fur. No one in his party paid any attention, because it was noisy down here, surrounded by a bubbling lava river and spewing geysers. Besides, they had just glided through the Great

Chasm on the back of a giant toad and were all in
windblown shock.

Rollo gazed fondly at his comrades and shook his
head in amazement. He still couldn't believe that
Ludicra, Crawfleece, Filbum, Captain Chomp, Weevil,
and ogres and gnomes he didn't even know had actually come to rescue him. They had crossed the Great
Chasm, going all the way to its sulfurous bottom. They
had braved enraged elves and fiendish fairies in the
Bonny Woods, and had gotten themselves captured.
Some had lost their lives, and all had risked their hides
to save him. Did any other troll have such great friends?

He glanced over at Ludicra, the proudest and most
amazing of them all. During her adventures she had
lost some of her charming flab; she wasn't the breath-
taking mound of fur she had been before. But there
was a grace and ease in her walk that was new. She
had always been confident in her stunning ugliness,
but now she had confidence in her leadership, too. In
her beaten-leather armor, with canteens, sacks, and
weapons hanging from her plump back, Ludicra looked
like a fierce warrior troll from some old myth.

We are writing history now, thought Rollo in wonder-
ment. Everything they had done lately would become
the stuff of legend. They had crossed the Great Chasm;
overthrown the sorcerer, Stygius Rex; and made friends
with a fairy named Clipper. Nobody had done any of
those things before! It was new ground ... just like
this bubbling slime they were walking through at the
moment.

'Hey, Your Highness!' bellowed Captain Chomp in

his gruff voice. 'We know it's your first time down here, but we've got to keep moving.'

With a start, Rollo looked up to see that the big ogre and most of their band were several paces ahead of him. Only Ludicra had drifted back to walk near him, and she gave the young troll an understanding smile.

'Chomp, he's tired,' said Ludicra, patting Rollo gently on the back. 'After all he's been through, poor thing.'

'Poor thing?' said Chomp, his tusks bristling. 'He sat around and ate rich elvish food while we fought our way down the tunnel. Did Rollo have to fly over a river of lava hanging from a bird? No!' The big ogre trembled at the thought of that dangerous feat.

'What's our rush to leave the chasm?' asked Filbum. 'Yes, it's not as nice as the tunnel, but there's supposed to be a treasure down here – the Old Troll King's treasure!'

'There's also a large band of elves down here,' said the female ogre, Lieutenant Weevil. 'With poisoned arrows. You remember them, don't you?'

Filbum twitched and rubbed his hairy rump. 'Yes, I do. But they had better stay on their side of the chasm.'

Rollo's sister, Crawfleece, hovered warily near her beloved Filbum. 'You're so brave, darling. But remember, the elves have been searching for the treasure for a long time, and they're still searching.'

'Pooh! That's *elves*!' said Filbum smugly. 'Trolls and ogres haven't looked for it yet.'

A small figure scuttled between them, and Rollo glanced down to see Gnat, the bald-headed gnome. He had hardly gotten to know Runt's feisty nephew because they had been fleeing for their lives. Runt was supposed to be running things back in Bonespittle, along with Krunkle, the master bridge builder. But who knew what was happening in the Dismal Swamp? Their old lives seemed so long ago, thought Rollo, like a strange daydream.

'We have to keep going,' insisted Gnat, looking up at Rollo, 'because we left the rest of the gnomes in the tunnel. We've got to guard that passage to the top . . . or hide it. Some of us can climb back up to Bonespittle, and some can search for treasure – but we've got to hold on to that passage to the rim.'

'Right!' answered Chomp. 'We don't want any more of those murderous elves invading our land.'

Everyone in the party agreed with that sentiment; then they looked at Rollo. He knew he would have to make a decision, although he had never seen the tunnel they were talking about.

'The story about the treasure came from Kendo, didn't it?' asked Rollo. 'He turned against his own kind. Even though he was once a fairy, I don't trust that enchanted bird.'

'Yes,' answered Ludicra, 'the bird told us about the treasure, but so did the elves by looking for it. They all believe there's treasure in this sweaty gulch, but where?'

Ludicra licked her blue lips and surveyed the murky red shadows thrown off by the lava coursing through the gorge. 'I would rather search for some leeches or grubs.'

'Ludicra is always practical,' said Weevil with a grin, 'and I'm getting hungry too. Maybe the elves fed Rollo, but none of the rest of us got anything.'

'What little food we had, they took away from us,' grumbled Crawfleece.

'Okay, we'll look for grubs as we go,' announced Rollo, although he figured that any crawlers living down here would be burned to a crisp. 'But let's go home.'

'Speaking of birds,' said Crawfleece, 'I saw a big one fly over us on the way down here. If the birds aren't our allies anymore, can we eat them?'

'We have to find something to eat,' insisted Filbum, 'because it's a long climb up those stairs. And we probably ate all the snails and rats.'

Rollo flapped his arms in frustration. 'All right, I already said we could look for food, but I don't expect to see any birds down here. I just don't want to get stuck in this place.'

'You can fly out anytime you want,' said Ludicra, gazing at him with her limpid, bloodshot eyes.

'Do you think so?' Rollo looked doubtfully at the sheer canyon walls, which rose up and disappeared into shadows and mist high above them. The upper rim and the lands of Bonespittle and the Bonny Woods were just a memory down here in the fiery depths of the canyon.

And where is our guide, Clipper? The resurrected fairy had helped them escape from the elves in the Bonny Woods, but where was she now?

'Ooh, look! *Worms!*' shouted Crawfleece, scampering out of the thickets into a dry wash filled with shiny black sand. In this hollow spot little white tentacles poked from the black soil and writhed invitingly.

'Wait!' shouted Ludicra a second before Rollo could speak, but they were both too late.

Crawfleece had no sooner lumbered into the sandy pit than she sank up to her plump waist in shiny black crystals. At once the worms turned into the slender fingers of a huge plant, which stiffened and shot plumes of sap into her fur. In seconds the troll was encased in a gummy white glue, and the tentacles wrapped around her like monstrous vines. They tried to drag her deeper into the sand, and Crawfleece screeched in alarm.

As usual, Captain Chomp was the first to swing his club, and his massive weapon landed with a splat in the gummy mess.

'Ow!' shouted Crawfleece. 'Watch where you're swinging that!' Even punching and pulling with all her strength, the big troll was unable to free herself from the clinging white tentacles and gummy sap.

Chomp lifted his club over his head, ready to swing again, but a vine rose up and shot a stream of sap at him. The goop struck him in the eyes, just above his snout, and the big ogre dropped his club. It landed on Filbum's foot.

'Whaa!' cried the surprised troll. As he began leaping around, clutching his injured talons, he stumbled over Gnat, who couldn't get out of the way fast enough. Then both of them rolled into the sandy pit.

Rollo heard a whoosh, and he turned his attention back to Crawfleece just as a big, mushy flap of fungus wrapped around his sister. With a strangled scream she sank deeper into the gleaming sand. Her head disappeared under layers of fleshy fungus and clinging strands.

Ludicra grabbed his arm, and Weevil started forward, wielding her big club. The lanky ogre bashed the plant several times, and it squirted sap back at her. But this battle didn't do anything to free Crawfleece, who was sinking deeper into the pit of blackness.

Ludicra and Chomp started forward to help her, but Rollo reached out to stop them. 'The lava!' he shouted. 'Clubs are no good. If it's a plant, it will burn!'

Chomp nodded and picked up his thick wooden cudgel. Then he ran to the smoking river of lava and plunged his club into the slow-moving stream. He brought up a flaming torch coated with dripping, fiery sludge, while the others rushed to do the same.

Rollo scouted the plant for vulnerable spots, but it was retreating deeper into the earth with its prize. To her credit, Crawfleece didn't go easily, and she resurfaced for a moment, waving an arm and gasping for breath. That exposed a bit more of the plant as it tried to smother her again.

'Hold on!' shouted Rollo. 'We're going to help you! If you get burned, I'm sorry—'

Chomp rushed to his side, his gooey, flaming club burning brightly. Rollo pointed to an exposed bit of white fungus flesh. 'There!'

The big ogre stuck his burning club into the plant, and it recoiled and shuddered, spewing sap everywhere. The sap burned brightly, and Chomp spread burning sap until the plant finally caught on fire. The flames and smoke let off the foulest odor Rollo had ever smelled.

Soon the rest of the party was also attacking the

plant with lava, and they found that the sap and strands burned very quickly. Crawfleece was able to break away from the burning tentacles, and Filbum waded into the flames to grab his beloved. Rollo and everyone else reached down to help them out.

They didn't finish until they had set the entire plant ablaze; then they rooted it out of the black sand. When they were done, they had barbecued fungus for dinner.

'That was a hard-won meal,' muttered Crawfleece as Filbum gently applied gizzard grease to her burns. She smiled at his tender treatment. 'But my Filbum saved me.'

'Actually, it was Rollo's idea to use the lava,' said Ludicra. But Crawfleece was smiling so sweetly at her beloved that she didn't pay any attention to the other female troll.

Rollo looked at Ludicra and shrugged his beefy shoulders. He just wanted to return home as soon as possible to marry his plump princess. To him, becoming king was less important, but he knew that would happen, too, when they got home. But the young troll worried that reaching Bonespittle was going to be a lot harder than his comrades had thought.

Captain Chomp inspected the blackened tip of his club and snorted. 'The fire river has made the wood harder. That's good! So, Rollo, should we rest for a time or keep moving?'

Everyone turned their attention to the young troll.

Rollo gazed upward into the smelly fog and he wondered if it was day or night on the world above. All he saw was shadow and mist because sunlight only penetrated into the Great Chasm for a brief time every day, when it was noon with the sun directly overhead. The rest of the time all they had for light was the eerie red glow of the lava river. 'Our stomachs are full now, but we'll still need food and water for later,' he answered.

From high overhead came the distant rumble of thunder. A few seconds later raindrops splattered upon them, followed by a deluge of rain that soaked them to their mangy fur. The lava river hissed and sputtered as the raindrops struck, sending up clouds of steam to join the fog.

'There's your water,' said Chomp with a laugh.

'We could also capture water from the geysers,' suggested Rollo. 'I really think we should—'

'Oooh, look! Worms!' shouted Crawfleece. She brushed away Filbum's paw and scurried along the muddy ground.

Rollo groaned. 'Sister, we went through that before.'

'No, they're real worms!' cried Gnat, who was closer to the ground than anyone. 'The rain is bringing them out!' The little gnome began to gobble the crawlers as swiftly as he could snatch them up.

'Wait, wait!' ordered Rollo. 'Don't eat them – collect them! We need the food for the climb.'

So the mighty band of warriors gathered worms for some time, storing them in pockets and knapsacks. Everyone ate a few as a quick snack. Then they kept gathering worms as they slogged through the mud, rain, and steam, and they had quite a supply by the time they reached a low archway in the canyon wall.

'There's the tunnel!' cried Gnat, who was scouting ahead of them. The little gnome dashed through the rain and peered into the dark opening, but he didn't enter.

As Rollo and the others approached the archway, Gnat ran back to them. 'Something is wrong,' said the gnome worriedly. 'We left gnomes to make repairs, but where are they?'

'Maybe they're somewhere higher up,' answered Weevil. 'It's a long climb.'

'But they should be waiting here,' insisted Gnat. 'I expected them to be here to meet us. We haven't been gone that long.'

Rollo walked over to the crude opening and looked around. He found a few arrows and the remains of a broken shield. 'Did you have a battle here?'

'Yes, we did,' answered Chomp proudly. 'And we sent those wicked elves running.'

'Could the elves have come back,' asked Rollo, 'to chase our comrades up the stairs?'

'The gnomes might hide,' agreed Captain Chomp, stroking a slimy tusk. 'The elves don't like being underground. Besides, the stairwell is narrow here, and we had the high ground. Even a few gnomes with shields could hold this tunnel against an army of elves.'

'Then what made them leave?' Rollo bent down and peered into the opening. Without a torch all he could see in the red glow from the lava was a passageway and two stairs – the rest was bathed in gloomy shadows.

'I'll go find them,' growled Captain Chomp, marching

toward the tunnel. 'You stay here, find a puddle of water, and fill our canteens.'

'I'm coming too,' announced his fellow ogre, Weevil. 'Lead the way, Captain.'

'Hold on,' said Rollo, shaking his drenched head. 'We're not going to split up the band. All of us will go and look just a short way. Maybe they left some sign as to where they went.'

'It will be good to get out of the rain,' said Ludicra. She shivered but gave Rollo an encouraging smile.

'We'll need light,' said Crawfleece, pointing to the lava. Once again, Chomp and Weevil plunged their clubs into the river of molten rock and made instant torches.

With the ogres leading the way and Gnat and Filbum at the rear, they headed into the tunnel and started up the slimy steps. Rollo had never seen this passageway before, although Ludicra and the others had not stopped talking about it. According to Filbum it was like paradise – dark and cool, with plenty of mushrooms and slugs to eat. They had found mysterious ruins, huge monsters, fake treasure, deadly traps, and other marvels. No wonder they were anxious to get back into the long stairwell.

They had climbed about a hundred steps. *It looks no different up there than down below*, thought Rollo. He saw a few more arrows, but little else of interest, and it seemed as if they could climb in this peaceful place the rest of their lives. 'Gnat, how old is this secret passageway?' he asked.

'Real old,' answered the gnome. 'Since the days of

the Old Troll King. And no one in Bonespittle remembers that ... except maybe Stygius Rex. I always thought the passage to the bottom was a myth, until Ludicra found it.'

Rollo glanced at his beloved, who was also looking at him. He was about to thank her again, when he heard stone grinding on stone. That dreadful noise was followed by a loud thud that shook the whole tunnel. There were several more loud thuds, and everyone stopped to look at Rollo. The noises were clearly somewhere above them, but the light from their torches didn't reach very far. Another thud sounded, then another, and the noises were getting louder and more ominous.

'I think I'll fill the canteens,' said Filbum, rushing back down the steps.

'I'll help him!' squeaked Gnat, starting his retreat.

The whole place was shaking now, like an earthquake, and dust fell on them from the ceiling. As the thuds grew closer and louder, Chomp raised his torch and peered into the darkness ahead of them. 'It sounds like a trapdoor,' muttered the ogre. 'Or maybe —'

Chomp's eyes grew wide, and he yelled, 'A boulder!'

Out of the shadows hurtled a huge rock, bouncing down the stairs, heading straight for them!

TWO

The Future King

'Chomp!' yelled Rollo as the mammoth boulder careered down the steps, heading straight toward the big ogre. 'Look out!'

Instead of pressing against the side of the tunnel to escape injury, Chomp lowered his shoulder and met the rock head on. It smashed into the ogre, crunching his torch, but he managed to keep on his feet and stop the boulder. Grunting, he held it against the wall. 'Get out!' croaked Chomp. 'Hurry!'

'Run!' shouted Rollo, knowing Chomp was risking his life to save them all. When Weevil didn't move, he shouted again, 'That's an order!'

Crawfleece and Ludicra were jumping down the stairs, following Filbum and Gnat, who were already gone. Reluctantly, Weevil followed them, and Rollo followed her. He could hear the stone grating against the tunnel wall as it tried to keep rolling down. Only Chomp's immense strength kept them all from being crushed.

They reached the bottom and ducked outside into the red glow of the lava river. Rollo skidded to a stop and turned to yell into the tunnel, 'Chomp, we're all out! Let it go!'

He heard more grinding; then the loud thumping started again. Rollo just managed to get out of the way before the boulder came roaring straight down the stairwell. It smashed into the opening and punched out a large chunk of the rock at the same time that it split into three chunks. One of the chunks kept bouncing straight ahead until it plopped into the lava river and melted with a sizzle and several loud pops.

Rollo waved to his companions, but they were already right behind him as he ran up the staircase. 'Slow down!' called Ludicra. 'Somebody up there doesn't like us.'

The young troll did slow down a step, but he wanted to reach Chomp as soon as possible. The grizzled ogre had taken the full force of the boulder to save the rest of them. He had to be badly injured . . . or worse. Rollo couldn't be very cautious, because Weevil and Crawfleece were on his tail, huffing mightily as they ran up the steps. Weevil still had her torch, although the light was flickering and weak.

Crawfleece gasped when they got close enough to see the lump of fur lying on the steps, bloodied and broken. Although one of his eyes was swollen shut, the other eye was open, and Captain Chomp groaned as Rollo approached. The smashed ogre could barely lift his head, but he croaked, 'Our enemies are scared to show themselves. Let's chase them . . . urrgh.' The wind seemed to go out of him, and the ogre fainted.

Ludicra moved past them and went farther up the stairs, her club in her hand. 'I'll guard this way,' she said. 'Get him out . . . quickly.'

'Take my torch,' said Weevil, tossing it to Gnat. 'Lift him onto my back.'

Crawfleece and Rollo gripped the unconscious ogre, who felt like two tons of fur, flab, muscle, and bone. With considerable difficulty, and cautious of his broken bones, they lifted him onto the other ogre's back. Weevil grunted from the weight, but her legs didn't buckle. She grasped Chomp's arms around her neck and set off at a steady pace down the stairs, carrying her comrade.

Then came the rush of tiny wings and a demented giggle, followed by a sinister laugh. 'Yes, you'd better hurry! You'd better run!' said a snide but familiar voice.

Clipper!

'Did you like playing catch with the rock?' asked the voice. 'What about *this*?'

The crude stairway lit up like a chimney, and a fireball came streaking toward them. It careered off the walls and shot sparks everywhere, and Ludicra barely had time to duck before it zoomed past her. Rollo dove for the steps, but the blazing ball still singed one of his floppy ears before it roared past. It shot between Weevil's legs and smashed into the stairs with a shower of burning embers. Weevil staggered, but the ogre never dropped Captain Chomp.

'Hurry!' shouted Rollo. 'Keep going!' Weevil hefted the massive ogre and plodded down the stairs. *How can we out-race fireballs?* wondered Rollo.

'Stay where you are!' ordered a low voice from above them. The hair bristled on Rollo's neck, and he smelled the putrid presence of the only living sorcerer in Bonespittle – *Stygius Rex*! Rollo gulped at the realization that the wicked sorcerer was still alive . . . and just above them on the stairs.

The whirring of wings also grew louder, and Rollo thought he saw the fairy Clipper flitting through the shadows. The rest of the party ignored the warning and headed down the stairs, except for Ludicra, who stood bravely at his side. He wanted to run, but he knew that would invite a chase that he couldn't win.

I'm the one he wants to see, thought Rollo glumly. He thought he should tell Ludicra to leave, but he knew she wouldn't go.

Holding a torch, a dark-robed figure with a staff walked slowly down the stairs. Even though he wore a cloak, the torch lit part of his hawkish face, and Rollo could see a mass of warts, and pale green flesh as mottled as ghoul skin. Stygius Rex looked older than the ancient walls of this tunnel, and he had the shuffling gait of a dead man.

'I could kill you right here,' croaked the old sorcerer. 'Come to think of it, that's what you did to me. But thanks to my powers, I was able to overcome a slight case of death.'

Stygius Rex touched the hilt of the black serpent knife, which rested in a snakeskin sheath on his belt.

'It's that knife that brought you back,' said Rollo. 'Same as it did for Clipper. If I had guarded it better—'

'Ah, but you didn't,' said the mage with a laugh. 'I want to be nicer to you than you were to me, so I'll let you live. In truth, Rollo, I need your help. You see, I intend to return to Bonespittle and take my rightful place as ruler, but the trolls and ogres seem to think that *you* are the ruler.'

The wizard laughed at the adsurdity of it. 'A troll as king of Bonespittle – what an idea! Since you dethroned me, Rollo, *you* must put me back on the throne. In fact, you will personally endorse me as king of all of Bonespittle and preside at my coronation. That's the only way I can return with dignity, and the land can be united. We'll all be friends again after that, and there will be no hard feelings.'

'Trolls are not going to go back to being slaves and servants,' declared Ludicra with a snort. That made Rollo proud of her.

Stygius Rex gave her a regal bow and answered, 'You are right, of course. The life of the trolls will be vastly improved, I promise.'

'How can we trust you?' asked Ludicra.

'Because you've actually done me a favor,' answered Stygius Rex, taking a step closer. 'Thanks to Rollo's bumbling, there is chaos on both sides of the Great Chasm. The elves think that you invaded and escaped – and will invade again. The trolls and ogres think that Rollo is dead and that the elves are about to invade Bonespittle. Soon both lands will clamor for a strong leader to bring order, which plays into my plans perfectly.'

He motioned around the gloomy passageway. 'With this tunnel and more giant toads, we can easily transport enough troops to invade the Bonny Woods. We don't even need the bridge, although it would be nice to build it after both lands belong to *me*.'

'United in meanness!' shrieked Clipper, flying around the wizard's head, giggling insanely.

'What if I refuse to help you?' asked Rollo.

'Then you can stay down here and think about it until you give in,' answered Stygius Rex. 'I will be ruler again – with or without your blessing, young troll.'

Rollo looked down the stairwell into the distant shadows, thinking that he had bought enough time for the others to escape. Only he and Ludicra were still in danger.

'That's *your* deal,' Ludicra said suddenly. 'But *I* have a deal of my own . . . to offer you.'

Rollo tried not to look puzzled, although Stygius Rex certainly did. 'What could you offer *me*?' asked the old mage with a sneer.

Ludicra lowered her voice to say, 'I know where the famous treasure of the Old Troll King is buried. You remember him – he was the one who hired Batmole to make the Great Chasm.'

Stygius Rex blanched at the mention of the long-dead sorcerer and the legendary treasure. Rollo knew that Ludicra was on the right track.

'We'll give all the treasure to you,' she promised, 'if you'll just go away and let us live in peace.'

That offer actually caused the evil sorcerer to pause

in thought. *A tremendous treasure – a legendary treasure – and all I have to do is go away.* Rollo could almost see the treacherous thoughts going through his head.

'Don't trust them, Master!' warned Clipper. The foot-tall fairy landed on one of the steps and stared suspiciously at Ludicra. 'Especially this one. She would do anything to save Rollo.'

Stygius Rex rubbed his warty chin and said, 'You're right, my henchfairy, but they all say the treasure is down here. I can spare two days to see if she's telling the truth. That's all you have – two days. Return to this tunnel with the treasure in two days, or the hostages will pay.'

'What hostages?' asked Rollo nervously.

'These two,' answered the wizard with a sly grin. He snapped his clawlike fingers and yelled up the stairs, 'Bring down the hostages!'

Two ogres appeared at the top of the stairs, and they were holding a slumped troll between them. It was Rollo's old master, Krunkle. He was wearing chains and looked miserable.

'Master!' croaked Rollo, starting forward.

'Stay there!' warned Stygius Rex, holding out his hand. He opened his fingers, and a blazing fireball danced in his palm. 'You'll like the next one, too.'

He nodded at the ogres, who grunted to unseen guards farther up the stairs. A moment later another pathetic troll wrapped in chains was dragged into view, and Rollo gasped.

'Father!' Rollo started up the stairs, but Clipper flew in front of him. The troll sneezed and his feet got itchy, while the wizard wound up his fist to throw the fireball.

'Be calm, lad!' rasped the old troll at the top of the stairs. It was Nulneck, Rollo's father. 'You aren't in chains, Rollo,' he said, 'so get away from here.'

'Father,' said Rollo tearfully, 'you were right. There *was* an Old Troll King – the elves and fairies know all about him.'

'And his treasure,' added Stygius Rex with a greedy smile. 'So you trolls have your mission, and you have two days – bring me that treasure.'

'This is really low,' said Ludicra angrily.

The mage nodded his head. 'Why, thank you, my dear. You don't get to be the only sorcerer in Bonespittle by being a nice guy. By the way, I haven't thanked you properly for throwing so much fear into the Bonny Woods. The fairies are at war with the birds, the elves are looking for flying ogres, and their leaders act like fools. It's quite delightful!' He threw back his head and laughed richly.

He pointed to the ogres who were holding the beaten trolls. 'And don't get any ideas of turning these soldiers against me,' warned the mage. 'They work for Sergeant Skull and are loyal to *me*. Be gone with you! Return in two days with the treasure, or the hostages will suffer.'

Stygius snapped his fingers, and the fireball disappeared.

Clipper cackled wildly and said, 'Beware of things in the chasm that you haven't seen yet.'

'What things?' asked Ludicra.

'Be gone!' roared Stygius Rex, pounding his cane on

the slimy steps. The ogres began to grumble ominously.

Tears running down his face, Rollo reluctantly tore his gaze away from his father and Master Krunkle. 'We'll see you soon,' he promised.

Ludicra joined Rollo on the stairs and pushed on his back to get him moving. 'Come on, let's go,' she whispered. 'We'll think of something.'

Shuffling his feet and sniffing back tears, Rollo headed down the steps. He shook his head. 'You told him *we* had the troll treasure?'

Ludicra frowned sheepishly. 'I didn't know what else to do. I thought we could get away – I didn't know he was holding your father and Krunkle prisoner. You weren't going to take *his* deal, were you? Do you want to go back and tell everyone that they should make *him* king?'

'No,' muttered Rollo. 'But everything we fought for has fallen apart. Stygius Rex is back, and now we must do his bidding again. Besides, where will we find this treasure?'

'First we must find the elves,' answered Ludicra.

THREE

A New Plan

On the other side of the lava river three bruised, dirty elves crouched behind a rock. They watched worriedly as a handful of ogres and trolls – and one small gnome – rushed out of the tunnel. One of the ogres carried a wounded comrade on her back. The beasts ran as if another boulder were chasing them, but no more rocks came crashing out of the tunnel.

The frightened monsters didn't stop running until they reached the edge of the burning river, where the heat drove them back. The female ogre set the injured ogre on the ground while the others drew clubs and took up positions to guard him.

'What are they doing?' asked Fennel, the youngest of the three elves. 'Why don't they go home?'

'They tried,' answered Dwayne, the blond-haired leader of the elven band. He was looking for the heroic female troll he had met after their battle inside the tunnel. Ludicra was her name, and she had spared his life. But he didn't see her yet. That was troubling because she had gone into the entrance with the others – but she hadn't come out.

'Are they after the treasure?' asked Spree. The redheaded female tugged on his sleeve. 'Do they know we found it?'

'Ssshh!' cautioned Dwayne. Even though no one could hear them over the popping and hissing of the lava, he didn't want to take any chances. Besides, finding the long-lost treasure was not the same as getting it, or keeping it.

'Look, there are some more!' said Fennel urgently.

Dwayne turned his attention back to the tunnel on the other side of the blazing stream of lava. Yes, there were two more trolls coming out, and his heart leaped when he saw that one of them was the amazing Ludicra.

'She's safe,' breathed Dwayne with relief.

'Who's safe?' asked Spree. 'The treasure?'

'Yes, the treasure,' lied Dwayne. 'But somebody tried to kill those ogres and trolls, and they still look scared.' The blond elf wasn't going to tell his comrades that he was more worried about Ludicra than some stupid clump of jewels and gold.

'Look, they're talking,' said Fennel, pointing into the yellowish fog.

True enough, the visitors from Bonespittle were having a lively conversation. With the bubbling, sizzling lava between them, there was no way to hear their words, but it seemed as if they were arguing. At least, they were waving and grunting a lot.

'Should we stay and see if they leave?' asked Spree.

Dwayne shook his head. 'I don't think they're going to try again for a while. They're ugly, but they're not stupid.'

Spree shivered beside him. 'I don't know, but I don't want to meet *anything* that scares a troll.'

'*We* scare trolls,' said Fennel proudly. 'At least our poison arrows do.'

'What about that huge monster, the giant toad?' asked Spree, giggling nervously. 'That beast scares me.'

'Everything scares you,' muttered Fennel. 'Do you know what scares me?'

'No, what?' asked Spree eagerly.

'The thought that we might never go home,' answered the young elf. 'That scares me buggy.'

Spree cast her green eyes downward, and so did Dwayne. The idea that they might be stuck forever in this burning cauldron scared all of them buggy. He could tell that the trolls and ogres were also afraid of that fate.

'You two go back to join the others,' ordered Dwayne. 'I'll stay here a little longer to watch them, although I don't think they're leaving soon.'

'Are you sure we should go without you?' asked Spree, already moving away from the black rocks.

'Keep low, don't let the enemy see you,' ordered Dwayne. 'Watch out for hungry plants . . . and crazy birds.'

'Will do,' answered Spree as she slipped into the eerie red mist.

Fennel crouched on the ground. 'Don't do anything stupid,' he told their leader. 'We need you.'

Dwayne gave his friend a smile. 'Don't worry, I want to get home too.'

A second later they were gone, leaving Dwayne alone except for the trolls and ogres on the other side of the lava. He hefted his bow and pulled his sling of poisoned arrows over his shoulder. Then the fair-haired elf crept down from the rock and made a circle back to the crossing.

'You've got to leave me here,' muttered Captain Chomp. The crumpled ogre lay in the ooze at the bottom of the Great Chasm, bathed in the red glow from the lava river. He did look awfully banged up, thought Rollo, but none of the band really looked fit enough to continue.

They were all beat, from his strapping sister Crawfleece to the portly Ludicra. Troll, ogre, and gnome alike, they were weak and still hungry after eating fungus, which was hardly filling. Chomp was injured more than the rest of them, but the bruises weren't the worst of it – not after seeing Stygius Rex.

The wicked sorcerer was back in charge, and he was meaner than ever. Rollo's father and the master bridge builder were in his clutches, and maybe all of Bonespittle belonged to him again. Everything they had fought for – especially freedom for the trolls – all seemed pointless now.

'So you just go on without me!' groaned Chomp dramatically. 'Just leave me my club . . . and a little food.'

'We don't have any food,' said Rollo, gazing at the fiery red river. 'And we don't have anyplace to go. This is a huge gorge, and we don't know where to find the treasure . . . if it even exists.'

He glanced at Ludicra, who frowned and lowered her bulbous head. 'Don't you believe in the legends of the Old Troll King?' she asked with disbelief. 'That treasure belongs to *us*.'

The little gnome hopped between them and cleared his throat importantly. 'Not exactly,' answered Gnat. 'That treasure was supposed to go to Batmole and the sorcerers as payment for making this chasm. Since Stygius Rex is the only one left of their race, he is—'

'But the trolls suffered for it!' roared Ludicra, stomping her foot and making a geyser shoot off. They covered their heads as steaming beads of lava pummeled them, but Ludicra shouted over the noise. 'The sorcerers took their revenge on us, and now the treasure should be *ours*!'

'You have promised it to Stygius Rex,' Rollo reminded her. Then he snorted and shook his head, almost like one of the ogres. 'The question is not how to find some mythical treasure, but how to rescue my father and Krunkle. We have two days.'

Weevil grunted, and the hulking ogre pointed to the opening in the cliff face. 'We can't rush them by going up the stairs – they will be waiting for us. If only we could outflank them from above and come down to attack. We could all catch them, and then we might stand a chance.'

Rollo felt all of their beady eyes looking at him, and he shook his head. 'Oh, no! If you think I can fly up that cliff, you're crazy. It's a hundred times farther than flying across the top, and I don't think I could do that now. What are our other choices?'

'Well,' said Filbum doubtfully, 'you could go up or down this burning river. There's supposed to be a volcano at one end and a glacier at the other. But how long would it take to get there?'

'We have to make it look like we're searching for the treasure,' declared Crawfleece, shaking her fist. 'If that old geezer hurts one bristle on my father's nob, I'll pluck his moles out one by one!'

'I know how you feel,' said Rollo sadly. 'He's been a good father, and he was right about more things than we ever imagined. Listen, *I'm* the only one the wizard really wants. . . . Maybe I should do what he says.'

'You'd tell the trolls that you want us to be slaves to that old bag of bones again?' asked Ludicra in shock. 'I don't think your father would want that, Rollo. As long as you're alive, we'll have hope.'

'And that's all we'll have,' muttered Captain Chomp. 'We'd better have a plan, too.'

Worriedly Filbum gazed at the steep, misty cliff rising into shadow. 'I think any plan should involve getting us out of here.'

Rollo nodded thoughtfully as he watched the churning flow of molten rock. Fetid gases rose straight into the black sky, joining the reddish mist over their heads. 'Hey,' said the young troll, getting an idea. 'Do you see how the gases float upward? All that smoke rises fast, and if there was a way to capture it—'

'If you could already fly, it would make you fly a lot faster!' said Weevil eagerly.

Chomp's grumpy voice rose from the ground. 'How are you going to capture gases?'

'In something that stretches,' said Rollo. 'Like the sail of a ship catches the wind.'

'Almost like that creature we ate a while ago,' said Gnat with a burp. 'It's giving *me* gas.'

Rollo snapped his talons. 'If we could pull one of those fungus things from the ground, we could stretch it!'

'Two trolls could mount a good attack from above,' added Weevil. 'And now we have a second troll who can *fly*.'

All eyes and snouts turned to Filbum, who backed away under their expectant gaze. 'Me ... fly all the way to the top?' he asked with a nervous laugh. 'Rollo was right the first time – that's crazy!'

'And if you fail,' said Crawfleece, 'that's not water you're falling into.' She pointed a fat talon at the bubbling, burning ooze.

Rollo nodded and said, 'That's true, but we've got to try. I wouldn't mind playing that boulder trick on Stygius Rex. Let's find one of those stretchy plants. Captain Chomp, will you stay here and watch the entrance to the tunnel? Tell us if Clipper or anyone else leaves.'

'Will do,' agreed the injured ogre. 'Put me behind a rock so I have some cover.'

After they made Chomp comfortable, the band from Bonespittle explored along the river. Rollo took Crawfleece with him because if there was anything to eat down there, his sister would find it. Sure enough, the big troll spotted another patch of the wiggling white worms. This time they knew that the real creature was hidden beneath the sparkling black sand, and Rollo called the others to help.

They were very careful to approach only the edges of the sand pit. Rollo felt a little sorry for the fungus, but then again, one of these monsters had tried to eat his sister. At his signal they began to beat on the edges of the creature with their clubs. After a few seconds the ground trembled, and the thing stopped trying to hide. It pulled in its flaps for protection, and that was when Rollo gave his second command. 'Grab hold on the outside!' he ordered.

Everyone in his party, including little Gnat, reached down and gripped the rubbery edge closest to him. With Rollo saying, 'One, two, three . . . lift!' they yanked the white plant out of the pit.

The black sand cascaded away, and the little white tentacles wriggled frantically. With much grunting and staggering they managed to hold on and stretch the creature like a big sucker fish. The filmy being twisted and flapped as if it were trying to fly.

With his free hand Rollo pulled a coil of rope from around his waist. 'Weevil!' he called. 'Catch this!'

Keeping one end of the rope looped in his belt, he threw the other end over the flapping fungus. The ogre across from him caught the line and pulled it taut. 'We need another rope!' she shouted.

Ludicra unfurled her cord and tossed it to Filbum, and soon they had the fungus blanket under control. 'Not only can it capture the gas,' shouted Rollo, 'but it can fly on its own! Pull it away from the pit – toward the river!'

It was like holding on to a tent caught in the wind, but they were able to drag the fungus to the oozing lava. Then it began to writhe in terror, rising over their heads, and Rollo grabbed all four ends of the ropes.

When his feet lifted off the ground, Rollo squeaked, 'I think I'm going up right now! Who wants to go with me?'

He looked at Filbum and reached out his hand. The frightened troll tried to step back, but Ludicra and Weevil pushed him forward. As Rollo grabbed his friend's hand, he willed himself to fly, and the two trolls shot upward, tied to the flapping fungus.

They sailed over the blazing lava flow. The heat baked them like a hundred suns, and Rollo could see streaks of golden flame mixed with the red-and-black crust of the lava. He was almost surprised when the rush of noxious gases caught the floating fungus and lifted them higher. Filbum screamed with alarm, but Rollo held tightly to his friend, wrapping the ropes around his waist.

'I'm flying!' cried Rollo. 'But I'm not guiding us – the beast is. It's okay, as long as we keep rising!'

'Yeah, we don't want to go *down*!' agreed Filbum in a shaky voice. His eyes bugged out at the rippling sheet of fungus. 'Go up! Up!'

Rollo tried not to look down either, because they were rising through thick clouds that made him cough. Even though his eyes burned, the troll forced himself to look down. There he saw Ludicra, waving to him desperately. From the ghastly look on her face, they must have been quite a sight. A second later Ludicra and his friends were hidden by the distance and the layers of mist. Only the glow of the lava cut through the fetid fog.

Now they rose through shadows, and the troll saw another faint slit of light high above them. The blanket of fungus suddenly realized it was no longer home; without warning, it began to spin around. Rollo and Filbum were soon twirling like a pinwheel caught in a hurricane.

'Help!' shrieked Filbum, clutching Rollo's waist. 'Whaaa . . . I'm gonna be sick!'

'Fly! Fly!' shouted Rollo. But nothing he did could make their canopy stop twirling. The frightened troll saw the reddish smoke getting closer as they dropped from the sky.

'No, go up! *Up!*' yelled Filbum in a squeaky voice.

'We've got . . . to cut loose . . . of this thing . . . and fly!' stuttered Rollo as he swept past his spinning cohort.

'Cut loose?' cried Filbum. 'I only flew . . . a few feet off . . . the ground!'

'Don't let it worry you,' insisted Rollo. 'You've got to . . . fly!'

As the last word spun out of his mouth a mammoth shadow seemed to overtake them. Rollo looked up to see the fungus go as stiff as a board, just as two giant talons swept out of the darkness and clutched it. The young troll gurgled in alarm as a monstrous figure of legend – a winged serpent with blazing purple eyes – descended upon them. Filbum whimpered, but even he was too amazed to look away.

Yes, we're going to die, but what a death! Rollo realized.

The dragon plucked a bite of the fungus with its great beak and chewed thoughtfully, looking at them with hooded purple eyes. He had bronze skin that seemed like armor plating, a sinewy neck, and a tail as thick as a tree trunk. Rollo gasped when the great serpent unfurled wings that were like twin bridges.

The brute gave his wings a leisurely flap and soared upward into the shadows of the jagged cliff, carrying the fungus with him. Rollo and Filbum clutched each other as they dangled on their ropes from his talons. The bronze dragon blinked at them and yawned, paying little attention to the two trolls hanging on to his dinner.

FOUR

Up In The Air

'Uh, Sir Dragon, where are you taking us?' asked Rollo, straining to remain calm and polite as he and Filbum hung from the beast's claws.

'Don't talk to him!' said Filbum in a strangled whisper. The troll looked worriedly at the monstrous winged creature who was calmly gliding through the blackness of the Great Chasm. 'He's busy – just let him fly.'

The wind pummeled Rollo's face and flattened his floppy ears. Sure, it would be easy to ignore the fact that a dragon was carrying them away, but that didn't do much to help his father and Krunkle. This dragon was clearly the most magnificent beast in the whole world. It would almost be an honor to get eaten by him.

But I'm not ready to go yet, thought Rollo. *If the dragon could just be turned against Stygius Rex, that would fix the old wizard.*

Bumping against him, Filbum groaned. 'We have the worst misfortune! Just when we find ugly girl trolls who will marry us, we have to go and die!'

'We're not dead yet,' Rollo pointed out.

'No, we're hanging from the claws of a dragon over a river of lava,' answered the troll. 'Oh, I'll miss Crawfleece.'

Rollo looked up at the massive shape that carried them through the canyon. Its great wings carved the air with loud whooshing sounds. 'I thought I saw something big flying over us when we came down on Old Belch. Now I know what it was.'

'The thing that's going to eat us,' answered Filbum glumly. 'Oh, I'm too young!'

'He hasn't eaten us yet,' said Rollo.

'Hard to eat and fly at the same time.' Filbum checked the bindings at his waist. 'Of course, we could untie ourselves and plummet into the lava.'

Rollo shook his shaggy head. 'No, let's see where he's taking us.'

Into the darkness between the light above and the lava below flew the great beast. A lump of fungus and a couple of sorry trolls dangled from his sharp talons.

'They're gone,' muttered Crawfleece with a sniff. The strapping troll gazed into the reddish fog over their heads, and her beefy shoulders shook with sadness. 'Ludicra, do you think we'll ever see them again?'

The would-be queen snorted back her own worried tears. 'I don't know. It's a long way up.'

'Will you two stop feeling sorry for yourselves?' muttered Weevil as she picked up their clubs and their packs. 'They have their job, and we have ours. We're going to find that treasure, right? Or at least find the elves.'

Ludicra stiffened her spine, trying to remember that she was now the leader of their band again. 'Yes, and Captain Chomp will stay here and watch the tunnel entrance. Gnat, maybe you had better stay with the captain, in case he has to send word to us.'

The little gnome gulped worriedly and eyed the wounded ogre. 'You wouldn't make me run about this dreadful place by myself? How will we know where to find you?'

'We'll leave a trail,' answered Ludicra. She glanced around their lava-lit surroundings, then walked back to the pit where the fungus creature had dwelled. She picked up a fistful of shiny black sand and looked at her cohorts. 'Weevil, Crawfleece, get some sand. We'll sprinkle it along the way. You'll find us, Gnat.'

'I don't believe this is a good idea . . . splitting up,' squeaked the little gnome.

'It never is,' agreed Captain Chomp. 'But I will heal if I can get some rest, and four eyes on that tunnel is better than two. Don't worry, little pal, we'll be all right.'

Something horrible cawed high above them, like one of those giant condors. The females continued to fill their pockets with black sand until they had plenty;

then Weevil took out her bow and notched an arrow. 'Which way?' asked the ogre.

Ludicra glanced back the way they had come after getting off the giant toad. 'Let's go the other way,' she said, 'and see something new.'

Weevil nodded and took off, stomping a trail through the twisted plants and smelly bogs. Hefting her club, Crawfleece followed the ogre, and Ludicra took up the rear. She tried not to think about Rollo and the danger he might be in. Would he make it to the top? Or had he already fallen to the bottom?

Rollo can fly, she told herself. *He'll find a way to save us all. And if he doesn't, I'll have to save his shaggy hide again.*

Still, the plump troll couldn't get the worry completely out of her mind. As she tiptoed between reeking geysers and sticky thorns, Ludicra was careful to leave a trail of sparkling black sand.

Still hanging from the dragon's immense claws, Rollo was suddenly blinded by a flash. It took him several seconds to realize that he was looking at sunlight – real sunlight from the top of the Great Chasm! But that seemed very strange, because he could clearly see the red lava just below his dangling feet.

Wait a minute, thought Rollo with alarm, *the Great Chasm is not so great here*. They had flown so far that the bottom of the canyon was only a hundred feet from the rim. Not only that, but the chasm widened into a steamy swamp, where the lava ran hissing into the water. The swamp was dotted with black mounds of pumice where the lava had hardened.

Even though the wind battered them, Filbum was snoring beside him. Rollo shook his friend awake and whispered, 'Filbum! We're here – at the end of the Great Chasm.'

'The end?' muttered the drowsy troll. 'Don't be silly – the Great Chasm doesn't just end.' As his beady eyes focused on the sunlight and the rolling countryside, Filbum blinked himself awake. 'It can't be!' gasped Filbum. 'Where is the glacier?'

'By the looks of that swamp, it must have melted,' answered Rollo. 'Look, there's even a meadow!'

Sure enough, beyond the murky swamp lay a broad expanse of greenery, dotted with wildflowers. From such a distance it was hard to say for sure, but there appeared to be a small stone hut in the middle of the meadow.

'I say we get off here,' whispered Rollo as the wind knocked them around.

'G-get off?' Filbum asked fearfully.

'Yes, we don't know where this dragon is going, and he's eaten most of the fungus.'

Filbum craned his neck to look upward. 'So he has, and do you think he might start on us next?'

Rollo shrugged. 'Don't you usually take food with you when you travel?'

'The water looks close enough,' agreed Filbum with a gulp. 'And dry land's not too far away. Besides, we can fly.'

'That would help,' agreed Rollo as he tried his sharp teeth on one of the ropes. 'Let's start gnawing.'

When a troll starts gnawing, things fall apart quickly,

especially when they know the weaknesses of rope. The chasm and lava lay behind them, and the murky water looked shallow beneath them. On Rollo's signal they took a last chomp to sever the rope. Clamping their jaws shut so as not to yell, Rollo and Filbum plummeted from the dragon's claws, leaving the rope ends flapping.

Rollo grabbed his comrade by the fur of his neck and tried to fly, but they hit the water before he could even start. The muck was warm, like some of the springs in Bonespittle, and all his aches and pains began to feel better. Filbum bobbed to the surface and floated among the reeds, a big smile on his snout.

But Rollo was scanning the sky, and he spotted the big dragon as it lazily banked around. He shook Filbum. 'Get underwater – the monster is coming back.'

'Huh? What?' asked Filbum. 'What if there are suckers and snappers in this pool?'

'I'll take *them* over a dragon,' answered Rollo. He sunk down to his eyeballs and pulled his friend after him. After a moment only their ears stuck up among the reeds.

The dragon cruised leisurely in their direction, but he quickly lost interest in the search. Gracefully the giant serpent turned and flapped his monstrous wings twice, sending him soaring over the meadow. The trolls rose from the swamp to watch the magnificent beast go, and Rollo wondered whether he would ever see one again.

'There are leeches here!' said Filbum happily. He snatched one off Rollo's furry shoulder and ate it. 'You know, this swamp wouldn't be half bad if we fixed it up – put in a few bridges and lanterns. At least the water is nice and warm. I might even take a bath in this water.'

'We're a long way from our friends,' said Rollo glumly, 'and a long way from home. Let's get to dry land.'

Slurping on leeches as they walked, the two trolls slogged through the bog. Rollo thought he had never seen such a blue sky as the one over their heads, and the strongest smell was of flowers. This clearly wasn't Bonespittle, or the Bonny Woods, either. Once they reached dry land, they were in a lush meadow with yellow wildflowers and tall, silky grass.

It was hard to believe that nobody lived in this pleasant place, except for whoever was in the small stone hut. Since it was the only building in sight, they walked in that direction. As they neared Rollo saw that it was hardly more than a hollow mound of stones with a low doorway. A troll would have to crawl to enter.

'Hullo?' cried Rollo. No one answered but the wispy breeze, which brought the smell of some purple flowers on the hill. There was a small vegetable garden in the back of the hut, and it looked well tended. The peacefulness of the meadow made Rollo want to lie down and take a nap. But they had to keep going – they only had two days before Stygius Rex did his worst.

'Do we go in?' asked Filbum. 'I think I smell food.'

'I trust your snout. Go on.' Rollo motioned to the doorway.

Filbum got down onto his haunches and scooted through the opening, and Rollo quickly followed. They entered a simple room with a wooden cot, a table, and a stew simmering on a tiny stove. The owner was away but obviously hadn't left that long ago. From the size of things, he was probably no bigger than an elf. Neither troll could stand up, so they explored while crouching and sitting.

Filbum grabbed the pot from the stove, burning his palm, but that didn't stop him. He found a spoon and was soon sharing the bounty with Rollo. 'I'm sure they wanted us to have this,' said the troll.

Rollo nodded as he licked slop off his snout. 'I think they saw us coming and ran away.'

'Or maybe the dragon ate them.' In record time Filbum finished the last of the food and licked his thumb. 'It could have used some grubs, but the vegetables were fresh. So where do we go from here?'

'Good question,' answered Rollo. He gave a huge yawn that rattled the hut. Then he felt bleary-eyed and loose. 'Dangle me, I'm tired.'

'Me too,' agreed Filbum. His opened his eyes wide for a second, then pitched forward, landing half on the cot and half off.

Rollo thought that maybe he should stand up, but he couldn't. He tried to crawl to the door, but his body felt like a rock. He wasn't going to move unless someone rolled him. The troll barely had enough strength to fold into a ball and fall blissfully asleep.

For some hours Ludicra followed Weevil and Crawfleece down a rough path that ran beside the lava river. Sometimes it got so hot that they had to step behind the rocks to shield themselves from the heat. When they cooled off a bit, they would trudge onward.

Twice they climbed a big rock to scout ahead, but there was nothing to see but fiery lava and choking weeds.

Ludicra was careful to leave a trail of sand, and she borrowed some from Crawfleece when hers ran out. Still, she doubted that little Gnat could run all this way to find them. It was hard not to wonder how they were going to get out of this foreboding gorge of flame.

Then it began to rain upon them, and the water hitting the lava made a curtain of steam. It was almost impossible to see, and they couldn't walk far without falling into a pit or a flesh-eating plant. So the two trolls and an ogre sat in the downpour, feeling dejected. Chomp was injured, Rollo and Filbum were as good as lost, and the whole band was split up.

Ludicra wanted to say something encouraging to Weevil and Crawfleece, but what could she say? 'The rain has made it cooler,' she finally told them.

Weevil shook water from her woolly head and yawned, which showed her impressive tusks. 'Don't worry, Your Majesty, just think about our mission. What do you suppose it looks like . . . this troll's treasure? How would any of us know a real treasure if we found one?'

'Wait!' said Crawfleece suddenly as she peered across the lava river. 'Did you hear that?'

'What?' asked Ludicra. All she heard was the rain sizzling on the lava.

They listened carefully until all three heard it – very faintly and at some distance: hammering. Someone else was down there in the bowels of the world, making noise on that gloomy evening, or whatever it was. Someone was building something.

'The elves,' breathed Weevil, lifting her bow.

Ludicra touched her arm and said, 'It sounds far away, probably on the other side of the river. There, it's stopped.'

They paused to make sure the hammering was over. It was, but at least they knew they were not alone down there in the infernal chasm.

Shaking the rain out of his blond hair, Dwayne approached the opening in the side of the cliff. He knew this passageway led to the top of the Great Chasm, but something inside had chased away the ogres and trolls. Now there was no sign of the band from Bonespittle.

The elf paused in the entrance and looked around. He felt as if someone were watching him, but that was probably just his nerves. He peered into the opening, which had recently been enlarged by a boulder, and could see the first crude steps. Dwayne was curious about what was farther up the gloomy staircase – something that frightened ogres and trolls.

Perhaps a thing that is an enemy of them is a friend of the elves, he reasoned. So the brave elven leader bowed his head and slipped into the entrance.

Although fey folk could see well in starlit darkness, the total darkness of the tunnel was more difficult. Still, he was close enough to the bottom that he had the eerie red glow from the lava. That was enough to allow Dwayne to climb the stairs without torch or lantern. If there was something dangerous higher up, he didn't wish to alert it to his presence.

The elf drew his knife but kept his bow on his back

because shooting into darkness was pointless. His arrow tips were poisoned, and he could always grab one to use as a hand weapon.

Dwayne cautiously climbed the stairs, his soft boots barely making a sound. He went so far that the red glow in the doorway was but a memory; still he pressed on. Now that his eyesight was worthless, the elf used his hearing and senses of smell and touch. It seemed as if something foul had burned there recently, because the stench remained.

But he didn't really know he had company until he heard the slight fluttering of wings. Thinking it was a bird or a bat, the elf pressed against the stone wall and drew his knife.

'Prithee, kind elf, don't harm me,' said a small, polite voice. Dwayne peered into the darkness but could see nothing. 'I am but a fairy who has lost her way. And you?'

'You've really lost your way,' muttered Dwayne, lowering his knife. 'But no more than we have, my band and I.'

'How long have you been in the Great Chasm?' asked the fairy.

'Many months,' answered the weary elf. 'The only creatures we have seen are those trolls and ogres who went running out of here a while ago. Do you know what scared them?'

'I did!' the fairy answered proudly. Her voice lowered to a whisper when she added, 'I threw a boulder at them and made them sneeze. The big ogre – I tickled his feet until he fell down the stairs!'

Dwayne was glad it was dark, because he was frowning at this fairy's tale. A sprite couldn't move a rock like that, could she? Of course, the wee ones often exaggerated. 'What's your name?' he asked.

'Clipper! No doubt you've heard of me.'

'No,' admitted Dwayne.

'Even better,' chirped the voice as the fluttering of wings came closer. 'Do you know where the Old Troll King's treasure is?'

Now Dwayne grew suspicious. Why would the fairy ask about the treasure? *What if this voice isn't really a sprite's, but is some trick of the foul folk? No proper fairy would get lost in this tunnel,* he told himself. *There was only one way up and one way down.*

'If you find the treasure,' said Clipper, 'make sure you tell *me*. Only me.'

'I must be going,' said the elf as he started down the steps. He tried to keep his back to the wall and his knife ready, but it was difficult to walk that way.

'Clipper!' roared a deep, ominous voice from farther up the tunnel. 'Where are you?'

That was no elf or fairy, Dwayne decided as he began to run down the steps. He didn't even worry about the darkness – all he wanted to do was get to the bottom. He saw the faint red glow just below him, and he would have made it to safety, except for one problem: There was a living thing crouched low on the steps, and Dwayne tripped over it. As the lump cried out in pain the elf bounced down the stairs, and that was the last action he remembered.

FIVE

Visitors From Far Away

'What have you brought me now?' asked Captain Chomp with a big, toothsome grin that showed his tusks.

Grunting with the effort, little Gnat dragged the unconscious elf to their hiding place among the rocks. 'I captured one!' bragged the gnome. 'Even though it was by accident, it still counts, right?'

'Right,' answered the big ogre, getting up on one elbow to study their prize. 'You're sure he's still alive?'

'Not sure,' admitted Gnat. 'This is the same one who saved Filbum, I think.'

'The one Ludicra is fond of,' added Chomp with distaste. He poked the elf's rib cage, and the fair creature took a breath. 'I think he's still alive. Better get some rope to tie him up.'

'Got it right here,' answered Gnat, uncoiling his strand.

'What was he doing up there?' asked Chomp.

Gnat shook his head. 'I'm not sure. I just saw him go in and I followed him. When I caught up, he was talking to someone – I think it was Clipper. Then I heard the voice of Stygius Rex, and our friend began to run. That's when I captured him . . . by lying in wait in the dark.'

'You mean he tripped over you,' said Chomp with a laugh. 'I can tie him up. Are you going to find Ludicra to tell her?'

Gnat gulped. 'You mean, follow the trail of sand . . . all by myself?'

'That's why she left it.' The ogre gazed up at the sky, which was once again swirling with fetid fog. 'The rain has stopped – you should leave right away.'

'I have no food to eat,' muttered Gnat.

'Who said being a hero would be easy?' snapped the ogre. 'Be off with you!'

With a heavy sigh, the young gnome scurried in the direction taken by Ludicra, Weevil, and Crawfleece.

Rollo stirred awake on the stone floor of a crude hut, and his head felt as heavy as pig iron. Snoring peacefully beside him was Filbum, who didn't even notice that he was tied up. When Rollo tried to move, he quickly discovered that he was tied up too. Out of the corner of his eye he saw a spilled bowl of stew, and he began to remember what had happened.

We're in the house at the end of the Great Chasm, beyond the lava river and the swamp. We've been captured rather easily by a sleeping spell or potion. But by what fearsome creature?

As he lay there wondering, the troll heard a scraping sound. It seemed as if it were coming from the ground beneath him, and he craned his neck to look around. When he saw the little stove moving, he quickly closed his eyes. *Someone is coming from a trapdoor under the stove,* the troll told himself. *It's best to look as if I were asleep.*

Still, he didn't want to be killed in his sleep, so Rollo kept his ears perked up. He heard the stove finish sliding, then some laborious footsteps and a grunt, as if walking itself were tiring. The hut was so small that no one could walk through without touching the sleeping trolls, and Rollo felt a leg brush his back. After the feeling passed, he opened his eyes and saw a squat figure standing in the doorway, gazing at the meadow.

'I haven't had visitors in a very long time,' said an aged voice. Their host didn't turn around, but he knew Rollo was awake. 'I must say I'm surprised to be visited by trolls.'

'Uh, yes, we're trolls,' agreed Rollo. 'But we didn't choose to visit you. A dragon snatched us from the sky and dropped us here.'

The old hermit turned around, and Rollo saw a plain but elderly face with great sprouts of white hair coming from every wrinkle. He wasn't an elf or a gnome, but he was about elven-size. Stooped and frail, he wore the tunic and breeches of a farmer. 'You were plucked from the sky?' he asked with amusement. 'And what were trolls doing in the sky?'

Rollo decided that for now he would keep his ability to fly a secret. 'We were falling over the Great Chasm,' he answered. 'Before that ... it's a long story.'

'Had you fallen to the bottom, it would be a very short story,' said their captor.

Rollo forced a laugh. 'We were glad to get to the swamp. Say, where was that dragon going?'

He shrugged. 'Who knows the ways of dragons? They often fly out of the canyon, but they've never dropped off any trolls before.'

'Since we haven't done you any harm, maybe you could let us go,' suggested Rollo.

The hermit turned away from him and said, 'You create quite a problem for me. If I let you go, you may tell your friends, and I will have trolls overrunning my meadow. You can't stay with me, because this house is too small for the three of us.'

Rollo wasn't going to say anything about the trap-door and whatever space might be under the hut. 'If we go back, chances are we'll be killed anyway,' he said. 'We have a very powerful enemy.'

'Who is that?' asked the elder with interest.

'The sorcerer, Stygius Rex.'

Their host smiled slightly. 'Is that old fraud still around?'

'He was,' answered Rollo, 'until we defeated his ghouls and killed him. But then he came back to life, and now he threatens to enslave us again.'

'I think you had better tell me this long story of yours,' said the hermit. 'But I don't guarantee that I'll believe it.'

'Sometimes I don't believe it either,' answered Rollo, 'and it happened to me.' So he told of the bridge across the Great Chasm that Stygius Rex wanted to build. He talked sadly of Clipper, who had helped him defeat the mage – only to die and come back as an evil hench-fairy. And he talked proudly of Ludicra, Crawfleece, Captain Chomp, and his comrades.

Midway through the tale Filbum awoke, but he soon realized they were tied up. So the young troll kept quiet and let Rollo do the talking. Toward the end the old hermit turned to Filbum and asked, 'Did any of this really happen?'

'Ask Rollo to fly for you!' insisted Filbum. 'He can fly, you know. So can I, and we're the only flying trolls around!'

So much for that secret, thought Rollo.

'Go ahead and fly,' said the wizened being. 'I'd like to see that.'

Hoping to keep the upper hand, Rollo snorted at his captor. 'I'm not a trained gnome to do your bidding. I fly when I feel like it. If you want to kill us, then go ahead and be done with it. You'll be doing Stygius Rex a favor.'

Filbum suddenly realized the seriousness of the situation. 'Wait a minute, sir! We're not even half done with the story! We haven't gotten to the part about the Old Troll King's treasure.'

The hermit lowered his bushy white eyebrows at his prisoners. 'Do you know where the treasure is?'

'Filbum!' shouted Rollo. 'If he doesn't believe anything we say, why should we tell him anything?'

Their captor looked back out the door at the peaceful afternoon in the meadow. A bee buzzed somewhere nearby, and Rollo could smell the heady scent of the wildflowers. He was suddenly jealous of this old codger who wanted so badly to keep his pasture a secret. He didn't want any neighbors, even though his land was as vast as Bonespittle, and much prettier.

'I am going to take a little walk to think about it,' said the lord of the meadow. 'Do I want to get involved with all of you? It's a hard decision.'

'You are already involved with us,' Rollo pointed out.

The frail elder waved as he exited. He wandered slowly into a patch of lavender wildflowers and vanished down the hill.

'Quick!' whispered Rollo, squirming around so that his tied wrists were near Filbum. 'Start gnawing.'

'With pleasure!' Filbum opened his mouth, showing an array of sharp teeth that could bite through anything.

A few seconds later the ropes were history, and Rollo untied both of them. 'Think we can take the old loon?' asked Filbum.

'I don't want to hurt him, but I want to see what's under this house.' Rollo grabbed the little stove and yanked it aside, revealing a small trapdoor underneath. Opening the lid, he could see the top of a ladder.

'Look at that!' exclaimed Filbum. 'Can we fit in there?'

'I'm going to try,' answered Rollo. 'You watch the door.'

The big troll lowered his legs though the opening with no problem, but his rump was a tight fit. It took Filbum pushing on his shoulders for Rollo to finally drop through the trap-door and fall into the chamber below.

'Ow!' he cried, landing on his rear. Rollo cringed and looked around, and he gasped at what he saw. It was an opulent bedroom with a huge four-poster bed. A lacy black canopy and red silk sheets graced the bed, and flowery lanterns were hanging from the high ceiling. Antique wooden cabinets were full of clothes, and there was a silver tea service on a marble table. Ancient tapestries hung on the walls, and they depicted bloody scenes of war and torture.

Two doors led to other rooms, and he cautiously approached them. Through one door Rollo could see a strange chamber full of heavy iron machines, beakers, and shelves stacked with bottles and potions. A large design of many swirls decorated the floor, and the room had a ripe stench, like an ogre's armpit. Rollo had an uneasy feeling.

A loud thud made him jump, and he turned to see Filbum grinning at him.

'Phlegm-dangle, this a nice little hiding place, isn't it?' said the troll as he walked around. Filbum threw himself on the luxurious bed and stretched out. 'Why don't we stay here a while?'

'You're supposed to be watching the door in case he returns,' whispered Rollo.

'You didn't report back to me,' countered Filbum. 'I thought you were injured. What's in those rooms?'

'That one's scary and smelly,' answered Rollo with a delicious shiver. He pointed to the door he had peeked inside. 'As for the other—'

'Let me look!' Filbum jumped off the plump bed and ran toward the smaller of the doorways. He had to crouch down to get through, and as soon as he did, there came a blinding flash of light. Filbum's scream trailed off into a strange buzzing sound, and a whiff of acrid smoke hung in the doorway.

'What happened?' asked Rollo, rushing for the door. But a bolt of fear made him skid to a stop and bump his head on the wall.

'Ow,' muttered Rollo, massaging the knot under his horn. 'Filbum, come out of there.'

But no answer came from the darkness of the room beyond. Even when Rollo grabbed a lantern from the ceiling and pulled it closer, the light was unable to penetrate the gloom. It was as if there were no chamber beyond, only an endless pit.

'Filbum?' squeaked Rollo, fear tugging at his heart. 'Where are you?'

He heard a clattering sound, and he turned to see the ladder rising up into the trapdoor. Rollo was too stunned to move, and he could only watch as the trap-door slammed shut over his head. That was followed by a scraping sound as the stove was pushed back into place, trapping him beneath the stone hut.

'There he is!' said Gnat with glee and pride. The squat gnome pointed to the trussed-up elf as if he were the most horrid monster in the world. 'I captured him all by myself.'

But Ludicra's jaw dropped when she saw who it was, and she gasped. Crawfleece and Weevil glanced at the prisoner, then at the troll. 'Dwayne,' she moaned. 'He's been hurt—'

The young troll started forward and stopped herself because all her comrades were staring at her. 'How badly is the elf hurt?' she asked casually.

'Hard to say,' answered Chomp, propping himself up on one hairy elbow. 'He won't talk to us, but maybe he'll talk to you.' The troll jostled the dozing elf and growled, 'Wake up!'

Looking sullen and angry, the battered elf refused to open his eyes. He just squirmed and tried to turn away.

'Dwayne!' ordered Ludicra sternly. 'It's me . . . Ludicra. Can you answer a few questions?'

The fey being opened his eyes and looked at the towering troll, and his anger faded a little. 'I was captured on your side again. You can kill me . . . I won't hold it against you.'

'Good,' said Crawfleece, lifting her club.

'No!' ordered Ludicra, staring hard at Rollo's sister. 'We need an elf in our band.'

'For sure he would be the prettiest,' said Crawfleece, 'but why do we need an elf?'

Ludicra looked pointedly at Dwayne. 'To lead us to the Old Troll King's treasure.'

Dwayne smiled, despite the bruises on his face. 'What makes you think I know where the treasure is – or could lead you to it?'

'Because you elves wouldn't still be down here in this sweaty hole,' said Ludicra, 'if you didn't think you could find it. I talked to Melinda, the Enchantress Mother, and she told me she sent you down here. I think she must have given you some idea where it is.'

'You've seen the Enchantress Mother?' Dwayne asked, sounding impressed. 'How did *that* happen?'

'Untie him,' ordered Ludicra, 'and let him sit up so he can hear our story. We're going to tell him everything that's happened to us – and Rollo – ever since Stygius Rex decided to build a stupid bridge across the Great Chasm.'

'He'll run away,' protested Captain Chomp.

The other trolls and ogres muttered in agreement.

'No, he won't,' answered Ludicra, gazing fondly at the blond elf. 'He can't outrun us. If he leaves, we'll follow him back to the other elves, and he knows that. Besides, we've seen the elven band – they're that way, just up the lava river.'

At that news, Dwayne looked glum, and Ludicra added, 'We're going to make friends with the elves down here because we have the same enemy.'

So they untied Dwayne, and he rubbed his sore wrists while they told him all about Stygius Rex, General Drool, and the defeat of the ghouls. Rollo had led them to victory, and they needed him to unite Bonespittle under a fair ruler. They told him about Clipper, the friendly fairy who had been turned evil by the black serpent knife. Their visit to the Bonny Woods, the rescue of Rollo, the war between the birds and the fairies – he was amazed at all of it.

'And now Stygius Rex waits for us in the tunnel,' said Ludicra. 'He holds our master bridge builder prisoner, along with Rollo and Crawfleece's father. If we don't return in two days with the treasure, he'll do something bad to them. We have to defeat him and find Rollo – again.'

'Hmmm,' said Dwayne thoughtfully. 'This is a bigger mess than I ever thought. Before you caught me, I met Clipper and your wizard, so I believe you. But it's a long way to the top of this chasm – Rollo and Filbum may be dead.'

'That's true,' said Ludicra sadly. 'But that doesn't change what we must do.'

The elf frowned. 'I can't convince my band to give the treasure to this wizard . . . if we even had it.'

'Maybe not,' said Ludicra, kneeling down to face Dwayne. She whispered, 'But we know you have *fake* treasures, like the ones you left in the tunnel to slow us down. We also know that Stygius Rex has Clipper and spies who may be watching us. As long as we are searching for the treasure, the hostages will be safe. Won't you help us? Please?'

The slim elf smiled sweetly at the bulky troll. 'For you, Ludicra, I will try.' With a groan of pain Dwayne rose to his feet and pointed down the burning river. 'There is a crossing that way . . . some distance. It will be hard for those of your size, but we must get across to the other side.'

'Lead on,' said Ludicra. 'Captain Chomp, are you fit enough to travel?'

The big ogre groaned as he lumbered to his feet. 'Yes, but I'm not letting any birds or giant toads fly me across.'

'No, none of that,' Dwayne assured him. 'I'm rather banged up myself, so I understand.'

'Let's go,' said Ludicra impatiently. 'We're running out of time.'

Weevil helped Rollo walk, and Gnat allowed Dwayne to use him as a crutch. The little gnome seemed to feel guilty about injuring the handsome elf, and Ludicra couldn't blame him. She was certainly glad that Dwayne was still alive. *I only want him to help us,* she told herself. *We need his help.*

At last they were doing something, were going somewhere, and had a plan. *Just maybe,* she thought, *we can still save Rollo, Krunkle, Nulneck, Filbum, and the rest of Bonespittle.*

SIX

Falling Deeper and Deeper

Rollo crawled onto the canopy of the bed, which he had dragged under the trapdoor in the ceiling. After hearing the scraping sounds, he knew that the door was shut tightly with a stove on top of it. The troll was in a huge room under a little stone hut, and there was no way out except for the door Filbum had chosen.

He gulped at the memory of what had happened to his friend. Filbum had run through the doorway and disappeared in a flash of sparks and foul smoke. Was the dark portal a trap for thieves? More importantly, was his best friend dead, or just . . . gone? And who was the old geezer who had poisoned them and trapped them under his house?

The troll had yelled himself hoarse, but there was no one to help. Rollo knew he could always go through

the door where Filbum had gone, but that idea made
him shiver. Although he was tall, the ceiling was too
high for him to reach the trapdoor, even standing on
the bed. At one point he flew up to the ceiling, but he
couldn't push the door open when he was standing on
nothing but air.

So that's why the troll was crawling over the canopy
that stretched between the corner posts of the bed. The
red silk looked strong and almost new, so he thought
it would support him. Holding his breath, he inched
his way until he was just under the trapdoor.

The ripping sound started behind him, and soon it
was coming from all four corners. With a howl the troll
plummeted through the shredded canopy and landed
with a crash on the bed. With a bigger crash the mattress
and frame collapsed, and Rollo landed hard on the
mattress, which slammed to the floor. The canopy and
sheets fluttered down over his head, and he shook his
fist at the trapdoor.

Rubbing his snout, the troll rolled out of the ruins
of the fancy bed. He staggered to his feet, groaning.
That's the problem with flying, he decided. *It always takes
a couple of seconds before I can do it, and the short falls are
over by then.*

First Rollo dragged the broken bed out of the way;
then he brought over the marble table, two chairs, and
two cabinets. After many minutes of trial and error Rollo
managed to stack all this furniture. Then he began to
climb to the top. The first time, he lost his balance and
fell down with a thud, and the furniture tumbled on
top of him. But the second time, the determined troll

made it all the way to the top and got his hands on the trapdoor.

He pushed with all his might, but a heavy stove was holding it down. When he heard cracking sounds beneath him, the troll muttered, 'Uh-oh!'

That was a second before the chairs and the cabinets broke and dropped him on top of the marble table. His anger growing, Rollo staggered out of the splinters of wood and grabbed the heavy table. With the strength of rage Rollo threw the table straight up into the ceiling, and it chipped off a large chunk. The table banged back to the ground, hardly dented at all. 'Hmmmm,' said Rollo, panting, 'that works better than anything else.'

Over and over again the big troll hurled the heavy table into the earthen ceiling. After a long time of doing this, he had made his own trapdoor. After grabbing some kitchen utensils from the broken cabinet, he flew up and carved away at the hole, getting lots of dirt in his face. Finally he had enlarged the opening enough to crawl through, and he was back in the beautiful meadow, outside the stone hut.

Only now it was night. The moonlit meadow stretched forever in one direction, and it ran into the lava-warmed swamp in the other direction. 'How am I going to get back to my band?' he muttered. 'And Ludicra?'

Rollo ducked into the stone hut, looking for the elder who had deserted them. To no one's surprise, the wizened being was gone. The troll didn't want to leave his friend Filbum, or the dark portal into which he had vanished. But he couldn't stay here. His father and Krunkle were still in danger. *Everyone* was in danger with Stygius Rex on the loose.

I can fly some of the way and run some of the way, thought Rollo. *At least I can get to the top of the Great Chasm from here. I just hope I'm not too late.*

'Good-bye, Filbum, wherever you are,' he muttered to the soft night breeze. Then Rollo's feet lifted off the ground, and he flew slowly over the tall grass and tender wildflowers of the meadow.

Filbum blinked awake and looked at his new surroundings, which were a lot like his old surroundings. Somehow he had vanished from the basement of the hut at the end of the Great Chasm only to end up in another basement. Of course, being underground was not unusual for a troll, but this was a very nice hovel. He glanced around and could see wooden tables and shelves, full of dusty old bottles.

In front of him was a doorway and flickering torch-light. Behind him was another door – with nothing but blackness beyond. He heard footsteps out in the hallway where the light was.

'Rollo, are you there?' he asked meekly. 'Rollo?'

The footsteps grew louder. A big head poked into the doorway, and it was not Rollo, unless Rollo suddenly had a dull metal bowl for a head. Under the metal skull was a gruesome, grizzled face; a barrel chest; and bandy legs. Only one creature in Bonespittle looked like that . . .

Sergeant Skull!

'Hey there!' growled the feared ogre. 'What are you doing in this room?'

'I'm . . . I'm just relaxing,' answered Filbum cheerfully. He stretched out on the earthen floor, trying to look as if he belonged there.

'No trolls allowed down here!' snapped Sergeant Skull. 'Did you call forbidden name . . . "Rollo"?'

'"Hello!"' answered the troll quickly. 'I was just saying hello to you. Or is it "good evening"?'

'Stand up!' ordered Skull. 'How did you get here?'

That's a very good question, thought the young troll. 'I think I got hit on the head,' he lied, 'because I don't remember.'

'You'll get hit on the head, all right, if you don't come out.' To prove it, the grizzled ogre hefted a nasty-looking club.

Filbum hustled out of the room into the light of the corridor, and Sergeant Skull peered at him with rheumy yellow eyes. 'You make me think,' said the ogre. 'Do I know you?'

'I was under your command in the big camp at the Rawchill River,' answered Filbum, which was the truth. But he wasn't going to remind Skull that he was a friend of Rollo's.

'Blah!' grumbled the old ogre. 'Terrible nights those were – feeding trolls and training them to fight. Then you bad trolls go and kill all the ghouls. Bah!'

'That wasn't *me*,' Filbum assured him, even though it was. 'I've been hiding down here for a long time. I didn't want to fight ghouls and Stygius Rex – why would I want to do that?'

Sergeant Skull eyed him suspiciously. 'This is the old sorcerers' lair, far underground. How could you get past the guards?'

Filbum rubbed the knots on his head. 'Like I say, I'm a little uncertain of that. But nobody is living here now, are they?'

'Not since ghouls left.' Skull narrowed his eyes at the young troll and barked, 'You are loyal to Stygius Rex, are you not?'

'Oh, he's the best,' answered Filbum quickly. 'But he's dead, isn't he?'

The ogre gave a wheezing laugh. 'You *have* been down here for a long time. One moon ago the master return, uglier and meaner than ever. He going to fix Rollo and all those traitors.'

'Rollo . . . is he still alive?' asked Filbum.

'I doubt it,' answered Skull with a cackle. 'Don't know why I should believe you, but you look cowardly. My guards will make sure you go back to Dismal Swamp.'

'I'm sure I can find my own way,' answered Filbum, scuttling toward the stairs. 'Is there anything I should tell the trolls in Dismal Swamp?'

'Tell them get back to work!' growled Sergeant Skull. 'Their holiday is over – old times are coming back.'

'I'm sure they'll be glad to hear that!' said Filbum as he hurried away from the fearsome ogre.

The frightened troll kept climbing until he was back on the surface, in Fungus Meadow. He looked at the moon and stars and thought how amazing it was that he was almost home again. But how had he gotten here? The only clue he had was a terrible headache.

And where is Rollo?

There was no time to worry about that now. At least he had succeeded in getting back to Bonespittle, which was what he needed to do. In the Dismal Swamp, maybe he could find a few brave trolls who would go with him to the Great Chasm. And maybe there was still time to save Krunkle and Nulneck ... and to see his beloved Crawfleece.

I've got work to do, Filbum told himself as he hurried across the squishy meadow.

'You're joking, right?' asked Captain Chomp with a gulp. 'That's not the "crossing" you talked about?'

'It's the only crossing,' answered Dwayne, 'since we destroyed the bridge we had. You go across hand-over-hand.'

Two trolls, two ogres, a gnome, and an elf stood on the bank of the burning river. They stared uneasily at a rope strung between a black boulder on one side and a gray boulder on the other. It hung about twenty feet over the gleaming lava and was shrouded in putrid mists. In the hot breezes of the Great Chasm the rope swayed back and forth, and it didn't look very safe.

'I'll show you how to do it,' said Dwayne, moving toward the rock.

'Not so fast,' answered Weevil, holding out a claw to stop him. 'If we let you go across first, you could get away from us.'

The elf scowled. 'I already promised I would help

you. An elf doesn't go back on his word.' He looked at Ludicra for help, but the big troll knew that she couldn't take such a risk.

'Gnat, you go across first,' she ordered.

'Me?' squeaked the little gnome. 'That's a long way, and I have short arms.'

'You have short legs, too,' said Crawfleece. 'That will be good to keep from getting dunked in the fire.'

'We'll secure the rope,' promised Ludicra, although she wasn't sure that the rope would ever support the weight of a troll or an ogre. Even if it didn't break, it might dip too low into the lava, giving them all the hot foot.

'I'll go across after you,' said Ludicra. 'If I can make it, all of you can.' That was certainly true. Only Chomp probably weighed more than she did.

'I'll check the rope and the knots,' said Crawfleece. The troll set down her backpack and club and climbed to the top of the black boulder. She worked for a few minutes, then grabbed the rope and swung away from the rock. Crawfleece hung in midair for several seconds, not trying to cross over the lava. Then she let go and dropped back to the ground.

'The pitons are pounded in good and tight,' she declared. 'But I wish the rope were higher up.'

'Me too,' answered Ludicra. 'Okay, Gnat, you're first. When you get to the other side, scout around and make sure no elves are lying in ambush.'

Dwayne laughed. 'You don't trust us very much, do you?'

'I trust *you*,' answered Ludicra. 'And I trust the rest

of your band to stick us with poisoned arrows as soon as they see us.'

'Come on, Gnat, I will hoist you up,' said Dwayne. The elf picked up the little gnome and helped him scamper onto the black boulder.

From his new perch the gnome gazed worriedly at the bubbling, steaming stream of flame. 'I'm a digger, not a climber,' he told his comrades.

'We're already deep enough in the earth,' answered Captain Chomp. 'Get something sticky on your hands.'

Gnat reached under his hairy armpits and loaded his mitts with sweat. 'That's sticky enough,' he said. 'Here goes!'

The gnome grabbed the rope and swung off the rock. He hung there for a few seconds, working up his nerve, then he finally started dragging himself hand-over-hand across the river. As the rotten fog swirled all around him, he cried, 'Bligh me, it's hot up here!'

'Just keep going!' shouted Crawfleece. 'You can make it!'

They all started cheering for the little gnome, and he kept moving along the rope. The farther he went, the more the rope sagged toward the inferno, and Ludicra watched to see how close he came to the flames. As he neared the other side Gnat disappeared in the mist, and they were all twisting their paws.

'I made it!' called a tiny voice, and they all cheered, including Dwayne.

The elf looked worriedly at Ludicra and asked, 'Are you sure you want to go next? I'll feel terrible if anything happens to you.'

'I'll feel worse,' she answered, forcing a smile. With some help from Crawfleece the plump troll climbed to the top of the boulder. Now she could see where the hooks had been driven into the rock, and she could tell that a good job had been done. The rope looked thick and strong – the only question was how much it would dip into the dreaded lava.

No time to think about that now, she told herself. *It's time to go*. So she grabbed the rope and swung her bulk into the air. Since she feared she might get tired, Ludicra didn't waste any time hanging around – she headed straight across the hissing cauldron of fire.

Things went well for a while, but that was only because she was careful not to look down at the lava. It was blazing hot, but it was blazing hot everywhere in the canyon. Since she was watching the rope and her claws, she didn't know how low she had dipped until she smelled something burning . . . like fur. With a start she looked down and saw that her feet were smoking, and they were only a few inches from the moving fire.

'Wah!' cried Ludicra as she lifted her feet and tried to keep going. She could faintly hear her comrades yelling encouragement, but the hissing and popping drowned out most of their voices. Still, she kept moving and thought she was going to make it . . . until she heard a tiny voice whispering in her ear.

'Hey, this is fun,' chirped the voice. 'Do you mind if I watch you?'

Ludicra craned her neck and saw a white fairy hovering beside her. It was Clipper, the evil henchfairy! The creature's eyes blazed with mischief, and she gave a tinkling laugh.

'Does this tickle?' asked Clipper as she fluttered down and moved her feathery wings under Ludicra's armpit.

'Oh stop, please!' wailed the troll. The wings tickled mercilessly, but Ludicra tried to keep going. Now her feet were burning, her armpits were tingling, and she was losing her strength. Plus she was so shrouded in fetid fog that she couldn't tell how far she had to go to reach safety.

Just ignore it, she told herself. *Claw-over-claw ... I'm almost there.*

But the fiendish fairy clutched onto her chest, digging tiny fingernails into her fur. Ludicra tried to kick Clipper off, but swinging her feet only made her dip closer to the burning ooze. She began to lose her grip and, with every passing second, she came closer to a fiery death.

This crazy fairy is going to burn me up!

'How do you expect us to find the treasure if you kill me?' she demanded.

'There are a lot more trolls where you come from,' answered Clipper with a laugh. 'This is just too much fun to resist!'

Feeling helpless, cut off from her comrades, Ludicra stared death in the face. *At least it will be fast,* the troll told herself. *But I'll never see Rollo again ... or Dwayne.*

As the fairy tormented her, giggling insanely, Ludicra's talons began to slip from the rope. With a cry Ludicra plummeted into the burning river!

SEVEN

The Treasure Map

Oh, I'm not dead, thought Ludicra with surprise. Her back was really hot because she was hovering over the stream of flame. In front of her floated the fairy Clipper, who had tried to kill her a second ago. Clipper's eyes were also wide with surprise, and she looked paralyzed. At least her wings weren't flapping anymore, which meant that she should have been burned up too.

But no, they were both in some kind of strange state, hovering between life and death. Then she realized they were both floating slowly over the lava, headed for the bank. The troll was close to safety; she could see the firm ground just ahead of her. As soon as Ludicra was across the river, she dropped like a sack of mealworms onto the hard sand.

Clipper continued to float in the air, her wings frozen. '*What* did you do to me?' the fairy squeaked angrily.

'Not me,' answered Ludicra, staggering to her feet. 'But I know what I would *like* to do to you.'

Gnat came running up to her, a look of amazement on his scrunched face. 'How did you do that?' he asked. 'Can you fly too?'

'Not that I know of,' answered Ludicra. 'Something saved me . . . and stopped Clipper.'

'Ludicra!' bellowed a voice from the other side. It had to be Captain Chomp. 'Are you all right?'

'Yes, I made it!' she shouted back. 'Don't send anyone else just yet. Clipper is on the loose!'

'On the loose? I can't even move!' snapped the angry fairy. 'Let me go, or I'll make you sneeze until your brains explode!'

'How about if I grab you and see if you can breathe under lava?' answered Ludicra, reaching for the fey creature.

When her talons got close to Clipper, there was a flash of light and a sharp burning. 'Ow!' screamed Ludicra, drawing back her paw. 'What is going on here?'

'I can tell you,' said a strange, furry voice.

The troll, the gnome, and the fairy all turned to see a cloaked figure outlined in the red shadows and swirling mist. He raised his hand, and his long fingers curled inward. At once Clipper floated toward the mysterious presence, although she squirmed and flapped, trying to get away. A few seconds later the fey creature floated in front of the hooded being, and Ludicra edged closer to hear what he would say.

'You've been a very naughty fairy,' scolded the visitor,

waving a finger in Clipper's startled face. 'You were
about to roast this poor troll, just for your own amusement.'

'I'm evil now!' bragged Clipper. 'Live with it.'

The visitor lowered his head, and Ludicra realized
that he wasn't very tall. 'All your devious plans will be
in vain,' said the mystery figure, 'because Stygius Rex
is not even worthy of your loyalty. He's but a shadow
of a grand tradition, which is now lost, thanks to him.'

'What are you talking about?' demanded Gnat
bravely. 'And who are you?'

'Ssshh!' cautioned the elder. 'I must speak to this fairy
while the enchantment lasts. Be perfectly still, will
you?'

Now it made sense why Clipper was just floating
helplessly in the foggy air. This was another mage,
perhaps an elf like the Enchantress Mother. *No*, thought
Ludicra, *there is something very un-elvish about him.*

'Little fairy, calm yourself,' said the stranger, moving
his hand slowly in front of the struggling flyer. She
stopped flapping her wings and stared blankly at him.
'You will visit your master and steal the black serpent
knife, which you will bring to me.'

'Wait,' said Ludicra worriedly. 'Do you know how
dangerous that —'

'Do you want to be back in the lava?' he asked.

'No,' answered Ludicra.

'Then be quiet,' said the mystery mage, never taking
his eyes off the frozen fairy. 'Clipper, you *will* bring me
the black serpent knife. Do you understand?'

'I'll have to kill the master to get it,' she replied. 'It's his favorite thing in the whole world . . . next to me, of course.'

'But you want to possess the knife,' he insisted. 'You have often thought about taking it, haven't you? Surely you must know a way to get it away from him. Now go find him, and leave these trolls and ogres alone.'

Clipper cocked her fair head and stared curiously at the hooded stranger. 'How can you command me? Why do I want to do this?'

'Because you know you serve a fraud,' he answered bluntly. 'Stygius Rex is a sorcerer, but without talent or honor. Cunning is all he has.'

The fairy shrugged. 'He has gotten far by being cunning. All right, can I leave now to do your bidding?'

'Go!' he replied, waving his hand. At once, the fey creature dropped toward the ground, and she regained her wits just before she landed in a patch of thorns. Zigzagging in confusion, Clipper finally flew away.

'All right,' said Gnat, stepping toward the dark figure, 'who are you?'

'Nobody,' he answered calmly. 'I've been nobody for a long time. Say, your friends are worried – they're coming across.'

'They are?' Ludicra asked with concern. She turned to see the yellow fog drifting across the blazing river of fire, but she didn't see any trolls or ogres. Still, the rope was swaying back and forth over her head.

Gnat also peered into the mist. 'Be careful!' he called.

'Can we come across?' bellowed Captain Chomp from the other side.

Ludicra gazed up at the rope and saw that it was no

longer moving, then looked for the hooded stranger. But he was gone, faded into the mist.

'Where did he go?' asked Gnat angrily. 'He was standing there just a second ago.' The little gnome dashed into the bushes, but he quickly jumped back when a vine tried to grab him.

'You won't find him,' muttered Ludicra. 'He's gone. Do me a favor and don't tell the others about him.'

'Why not?' asked the gnome.

Ludicra shivered, despite the heat from the lava. 'Because I don't want to give them anything else to worry about.'

'But he saved your life.'

'Did he?' asked Ludicra, shaking her woolly head. 'For how long?'

It took another hour, but they finally got everybody across the fiery river, even Captain Chomp. Two ogres, two trolls, and a gnome stood waiting for a dazed elf to lead them. Ludicra felt certain they could trust Dwayne, although she was the only one who felt that way.

'We have to backtrack,' said their elven guide. Dwayne led them in the direction where they had heard the hammering, only now they were on the Bonny Woods side of the river. As they walked the ogres kept swinging their clubs, ready to bash an unseen enemy.

'Have you seen the treasure?' Ludicra asked.

Dwayne nodded slowly. 'From a distance . . . I *think* I have.'

'It didn't look like treasure?'

'You'll see what I mean.' Dwayne glanced at her and

lowered his voice. 'What happened to the other two trolls who were with your band?'

Ludicra scowled. 'I wish I knew. They wanted to get to the top, to surprise Stygius Rex from above. Now I wish we hadn't split up.'

'I know what you mean,' said Dwayne with a rueful smile. 'I wish I had stayed with my band too. A leader should never leave his followers.'

Ludicra muttered in agreement as she thought about Rollo. It was funny, but he had a habit of leaving his followers. *On the other claw, I try to keep them together,* she told herself.

The elf sighed and rubbed a bump on his head. 'Sometimes I think we will wander around in this fiery pit forever.'

'No kidding,' said Ludicra with a gulp. 'Why don't you leave? You must have a way to get to the top.'

'We haven't gotten what we came for,' he said grimly. With that, the elf limped along several more paces, his pretty face scrunched in thought.

'Treasure?' asked the troll, shaking her shaggy head. 'Is it all that important?'

'It's important to *you*,' he observed. 'It's important to Stygius Rex. My people are obsessed with it. It's so close, yet so far—'

'Draw me a map to get there,' said Ludicra.

He stopped to look at her, and Chomp, Weevil, Crawfleece, and Gnat also stopped. 'But I am leading you,' said Dwayne, sounding hurt.

'The other elves may have an opinion about that,' answered Ludicra. 'They may not let you. Also, you are hurt – if we have to run, you won't be able to keep up with us.'

'Run from the elves?' scoffed Captain Chomp. 'Don't make jokes, Ludicra.'

'This is no joke.' The chubby troll turned and looked down at the elf. He was so cute, she wanted to hug him like a newborn tree sloth. 'Dwayne, if you tell us where the treasure is and we are able to get it, I will give the elves half.'

'You can't make that promise!' snapped Crawfleece, shoving her bulk between them. 'We need that treasure to free the hostages!'

'Which we cannot do unless Dwayne tells us where it is,' said Weevil, pushing the big troll back. 'Let Ludicra make her deal – it will hurry things up.'

'No!' rumbled Crawfleece. The next moment the hulking troll and the wiry ogre were in each other's snouts, huffing angrily.

'Stand down!' roared Chomp, pushing them both apart. 'When Rollo is not here, Ludicra is our leader. Besides, any map drawn by this sneaky elf will probably be worthless.'

Ludicra snorted, because she knew they could trust the elven leader. 'Dwayne has dealt honorably with me,' she said. 'If he says he will take us to the treasure, he will.'

'Hold on.' The handsome elf laughed merrily. 'Before you decide how to spend it, you had better see it first. What do you have to draw on?'

'I have something,' said Gnat, taking off his backpack. 'We thought we might need to chart the tunnel.'

He took out a piece of bark and a chunk of charcoal and handed them to the elf.

'I will try to reason with my fellows,' promised Dwayne, 'but they may not want to help you.' As he drew on the bark the elf said, 'Here is the elven camp, and here is the river. Just march to the south until you see this pool of water. They sometimes come down there to drink.'

'They?' asked Crawfleece. 'Who are "they"?'

'They fly, come in all sizes, and will eat you,' answered Dwayne. 'As to what you want to call them, I'll leave that up to you. But you must climb sheer rock here – behind the pool – to even get high enough to see their nest. Try to reach this narrow ledge. Once you see their nest . . . well, you will know why the treasure is likely to stay there.'

He finished the map and handed it to Ludicra, who gave him a grateful smile. 'I . . . I will treasure this,' she stammered. 'I mean, it will help us find the treasure.'

Dwayne smiled back. 'Now that you have the map, it may be a good idea to let me go ahead . . . alone. Listen for our hammering so you'll know where we are. When the sun is overhead and there's light in the chasm, I'll make sure we're working in the boulders. You can slip past us by going close to the lava.'

Captain Chomp snorted and said, 'That would be a nice place for an ambush.'

'Yes,' admitted Dwayne, shining his brilliant blue eyes on Ludicra. 'But you are not going to get past a whole band of elves unless I help you. I don't think I can get them to agree to giving you the treasure, but I can offer you *my* help. If you want that, you'll have to trust me.'

'Trust you,' said Ludicra with a dreamy sigh. Crawfleece bumped her in the back, and she blinked with alarm at the attractive elf. 'Get moving!' she ordered.

Dwayne doffed his cute little hat to all of them. 'I won't forget your compassion. Good evening.' The elf limped into the noxious fog and was gone.

'Ewww,' said Weevil. 'Compassion? I think that's an insult for ogres.'

'She's right!' grumbled Chomp as he hobbled toward Ludicra. 'Let's just go smash their skulls! Then we'll go back and do the same thing to Stygius Rex.'

'Captain Chomp,' said Ludicra, puffing out her stomach to more than match his. 'We're on *their* side of the chasm now, and we'll visit them in peace.'

The troll looked worriedly at their gloomy surroundings and whispered, 'Captain Chomp, *someone* is no doubt watching us. Clipper was here, and I've also seen birds. As long as they see us searching for the treasure, the hostages are safe. Let's give Rollo and Filbum some time to do their job. Just in case, the ogres will put their shields up, and we'll all walk behind them.'

'Very well,' muttered the big ogre, lifting his heavy oaken armor. 'We move with caution.'

Some hours later the first angular rays of sunlight crept down the walls of the Great Chasm. Like a trapdoor slowly opening, sunlight flowed over the black boulders, deadly plants, stinky gases, and bubbling ooze. For a bright, shining moment daylight brightened the bottom of the fiery gorge, and the plants stretched upward and plumped their leaves. Dwayne held his finger to his lips – to keep his band of elves quiet.

'I see the foul folk!' whispered the scout on top of the highest rock. 'They just passed our position.'

An elf picked up his bow, and Dwayne stared at him. 'Let them pass,' he hissed. 'They have flying trolls, lots of rope, and more bravery than brains. Let *them* get the treasure for *us*.'

'Yeah!' said Spree, giggling. 'Let the trolls get it for us. Tee-hee!'

The other elves snickered in agreement, and Dwayne waved his hand. 'Scouts, give them a few minutes to get ahead, then follow them. Don't let them see you. The rest of the band, get back to work. Fix the ladder while you have daylight. Hurry!'

His elves scurried off, and Dwayne allowed himself a sly smile of victory.

EIGHT

Hovel Sweet Hovel

The Dismal Swamp didn't look much different from before, especially by the harsh light of midday. The swaying bridges, mounds of mud, old tree stumps, and slimy pools of black water all smelled like home. Filbum did have to go around a few bridges that were roped off because they were in disrepair. That would not have happened before the night Stygius Rex came to trollnap half the town.

All of that seems so long ago, although it has only been a couple of moons, thought Filbum. *Everything has changed, but it all looks the same.*

Of course, the bridges were deserted at this ghastly hour, but Filbum wasn't exactly alone. He had been followed all the way from Fungus Meadow by a pair of suspicious ogres. They kept their distance, but he could clearly see them in all this daylight, slinking behind him. These escorts were no doubt loyal to Sergeant Skull, who had crawled back to his old master, the mage.

Some ogres can't see the big picture, thought Filbum glumly. He wondered how his fellow trolls would see things.

His first stop would have to be the hovel of Vulgalia, Rollo's mother. She must be worried healthy about both Crawfleece and Rollo, plus her husband, Nulneck. Last time he had seen them, they were all fine, even if they were far away and held prisoner.

The young troll whirled around and considered the portal he had just popped through. It must mean he could return to that distant meadow, where he had left Rollo, if he could find his way back into the deep lair of the dead sorcerers. That wasn't likely, with unfriendly ogres everywhere, but it was a thought to keep in mind.

Filbum recognized the creaking of the old planks beneath his feet and knew he was near Rollo's home. On this spot he had seen Crawfleece drag a sucker fish out of the bog and wrestle it to their dinner table. On these swaying spans he and his friends had dodged ogre patrols and chased billy goats. Just a few weeks ago they were attending classes with Master Krunkle, and not listening half the time. That innocent period seemed so long ago.

The troll stopped suddenly at a section of broken bridge, and he had to go around. It was true: They didn't have any leadership in the Dismal Swamp, and everything was broken. The old ruler was off looking for treasure, and so was the new one, although Rollo was probably lost by now. *What can I do by myself?* thought Filbum.

I have to get a force together and take it to the Great Chasm, he answered himself. *So we can attack Stygius Rex from above – that was the plan.*

He reached a slimy mound where three bridges sloped off, and he knew that Rollo and Crawfleece lived under this grimy hillock. Hanging on to vines and old tree roots, Filbum swung under the bridge and planted his feet only a few inches from the brackish water. There he found the old wooden door and knocked as quietly as he could. 'Vulgalia?' he whispered. 'I know it's the middle of the day, but please let me in!'

'Go away!' rasped a voice. 'Haven't I suffered enough?'

'I just left Rollo and Crawfleece,' he answered. 'It's me . . . Filbum!'

'Filbum? Just a moment.' He heard the bolt slipping back, and the door opened a crack as suspicious eyes stared out. Vulgalia looked thinner and shorter, compared with the days before the big revolt, and her eyes looked redder than usual.

'Come in! Hurry!' she whispered, dragging him into the hovel. Vulgalia slammed and bolted the door shut behind him; then she glared at him. 'Are they still alive?'

'Yes!' answered Filbum.

'Good, then I'll be able to kill them when they get home.' The worried mother began to pace her cramped quarters, and Filbum looked around. He had hoped to smell home cooking, because Vulgalia could do wonders with slugs and grubs. But the pots were cold, and the mud hovel seemed gloomier than usual.

'We've got to get a large force of trolls to march on the Great Chasm!' said Filbum excitedly. 'To save your husband, Nulneck, and Krunkle.'

The old troll fixed him with a jaundiced eye. 'Just a second. Three-fourths of my family have gone to the Great Chasm, and none of them have come home yet. So you want to send *more* trolls to go after them?'

'But they're all right!' insisted Filbum. 'Your family is okay – they just need help. Do the trolls still meet and talk to one another?'

Vulgalia snorted. 'That's all there is to do. Every night we stand around and wonder what is going to happen to us. Are you going to tell me what's going on?'

Filbum sighed. 'It's a really long story, but let's just say that we have to kill Stygius Rex ... again! He's holding Nulneck and Krunkle in the tunnel that leads to the bottom of the Great Chasm. We need to attack him from above, while the others attack from the bottom. Can you get a group together?'

'Why can't you?' she asked suspiciously.

'I'm afraid they're following me,' answered the troll, looking over his shoulder.

'So you led them here,' muttered Vulgalia. The troll sighed heavily. 'All right, I'll lead a band to the Great Chasm. The things a mother does for her family!'

She shoved him toward the door. 'Now you had better go into hiding and leave me alone.'

'I'll meet you at the rim of the chasm,' promised Filbum, although he didn't know how he was going to get there.

Vulgalia opened the door and pushed him out into the daylight. The young troll almost stepped into the swirling black water, but he jumped back just in time. He had forgotten how to walk in the swamp, and he looked for tentacles in the silty ooze. But even the sucker fish were too lazy to work on this overly bright day.

He climbed up to the bridge, and the sun glinted off something very shiny – right into his eyes. Filbum staggered backward and almost fell off the bridge back into the muck, but strong arms caught him. Then those strong arms whirled him around and pinned him facedown in the mud at the top of the bridge. The poor troll was still blinded from the bright flash of light, and he couldn't see who had captured him. But they smelled like ogres.

Daylight shimmered off the shiny object again, and he saw what it was – Sergeant Skull's head. The new captain of the guard had been following the troll himself, along with a comrade.

'Why are you bothering me?' asked Filbum, squirming around. 'You told me to go home, and I did.'

The ogre crossed his brawny arms and clicked his tusks. 'I went back to check that dungeon you came from, little troll. That's a secret portal . . . or something bewitched.'

'Heh-heh,' Filbum laughed nervously. 'I forgot to mention that, because I had a headache. Now that we have cleared that up, can I go?'

'Not so fast,' rasped Skull. 'Then I remembered who you are. You are Filbum, friend of Rollo's. You were a good troll – before you became a traitor.'

Now there's no way to lie, thought Filbum with alarm. He hated to tell the truth, but Sergeant Skull looked like an ogre who was out for himself. Filbum sighed with defeat. 'All right, I suppose you will want part of the treasure to let me go.'

The metal bowl on Skull's head came down a notch. 'What treasure?'

'Oh, don't play coy with me,' said Filbum. 'A smart ogre like you – surely you know where Stygius Rex has been all this time. I mean, he and Clipper. You know, he likes that henchfairy better than all of you ogres combined.'

Sergeant Skull looked at his fellow ogre. 'Gouge, choke him until he starts talking about the treasure.'

'Treasure! Treasure!' shouted Filbum as the grip got tighter around his neck. 'I'm surprised you don't know about it already. Stygius Rex sure knows, and so do all the elves and fairies in the Bonny Woods.'

'How do you know so much about Stygius Rex?' asked Skull with a snarl.

'I just saw him,' said Filbum. 'We just left a meeting with His Mage-ship. He has Clipper with him, and some ogres from your command. I even saw the hostages . . . Krunkle and Nulneck.'

Now the grizzled ogre blinked in amazement at Filbum, and he motioned to his underling. 'Let him go. He knows too much for it not to be true.'

Filbum shook his head sadly. 'So His Fireballness didn't tell you about the treasure. Seems as if he wants to cut you out.'

Sergeant Skull grabbed the troll by the hairy scruff of his neck and barked, 'You tell me now.'

The troll smiled sympathetically. 'We've all had a poor education. Stygius Rex didn't tell us about our real history. Go back about a thousand years, and there was an Old Troll King who ruled Bonespittle. There were many sorcerers back then, and they mostly kept to themselves.'

Filbum scratched a hairy mole. 'Hmmmm, that makes me wonder about the old guy in the stone hut. Oh, never mind . . . back a thousand years, we were always fighting with the fey folk of the Bonny Woods. So the Troll King hired a sorcerer named Batmole to make the Great Chasm to keep the lands apart. That's where the treasure comes in.'

He basically told the ogre chief the truth, leaving out a few parts. When Filbum finished, he laughed. 'So do you think Rollo and I went to all this trouble – all those trips to the Bonny Woods – for the title of king? Hardly! We were just looking for the treasure. Stygius Rex is looking for the treasure, the elves are looking for it, *everyone* is looking for it. The only one who's not looking for it is *you*.'

'Yeah,' growled Sergeant Skull. 'What's the matter with me?'

Filbum shook his head thoughtfully. 'The one who gets the treasure will be the real king of Bonespittle. You could *pay* soldiers – what an army you would have! It wasn't very fair for Stygius Rex to keep you out of the hunt. After all, you're the only fighting force he has.'

Skull snorted loudly. 'Yeah, what's with that? Without me, he's just a well-dressed corpse.'

'Of course, if you want a partner,' said Filbum, 'I've seen the treasure, and I know the secret passage to the bottom. It so happens that my previous partners deserted *me*, so we're in the same bog.'

Sergeant Skull put his arm around Filbum's shoulders, and his breath was like a burst of swamp gas. 'You're my new partner. I like you because you've switched to the winning side. This time the winning side is Sergeant Skull's.' He lowered his voice and added, 'I have horses hidden in the forest.'

'Horses,' said the troll, licking his lips. 'Uh . . . can we have breakfast before we go?'

The ogre motioned to his underling. 'Gouge, give him food. We'll eat while we march.'

Filbum smiled because he was already liking this new arrangement. Maybe he should have told them about the dragon, but he had left that part out. At least now he knew how he was going to get back to the Great Chasm . . . and his friends.

Rollo slipped off his feet and slid down the hill on a wave of tiny pebbles. He rolled into a briar patch and jumped up, brushing the thorns off his hide. For the third time he had failed to reach the rim of the Great Chasm at its shortest distance, where it was just a hill. Behind him lay the dense mist of the swamp, where the fiery lava ran into murky water and stopped.

I can fly! Rollo told himself, but the troll had been trying to fly for hours – with no success. He concentrated and visualized himself swooping over the hill and landing miles away, near his friends. But it was no good – he could barely jump.

From the stone hut in the meadow he had flown a short distance. But he didn't fly very fast, and it seemed easier to walk. After walking all day and thinking too much, Rollo had tried to fly again. That was when he had failed, and he had been walking ever since. Somehow he had lost his power in this steamy wilderness at the end of the world.

Hunger, he realized. *I must be too hungry to fly.* But hunger had never stopped him before. When he had been hanging for days in that giant spiderweb, he had still been able to fly a little. It was as if all the magic had left him, along with his friends and his confidence. Now he was just like any troll, except that he was so lonely.

Maybe the magic has finally worn off, he told himself, sitting in the mud at the edge of the swamp. Stygius Rex had said his magic was contagious, but he didn't say it would last forever. When Rollo started feeling sorry for himself – for being so far away from his family and Ludicra – that was when the magic had left him.

Taking a deep breath, Rollo stared hard at the sandy hill that had defeated him three times. *If I can just climb that nob, I can see the land all around me. And I'll be on top of the chasm, the mission Filbum and I set out to accomplish.* Thinking of his friend made the big troll gulp with grief. Then he looked back at the hill.

He had trudged through the swamp to get there, and he could backtrack many miles to where it was more level. But Rollo was too tired to turn back. It was up and over.

He dug in his talons and barreled up the rocky incline. He charged until the soil turned to sand and his leg muscles roared in pain. The troll fell to his stomach and began to crawl, swimming furiously in the shifting sand dune. Awkwardly he squirmed upward until he reached eye level with the top of the dune, and from there he caught a glimpse of a bright light glowing among the brambles. It was like a lamp shining in a dark tunnel, even though it was already daylight.

This sight inspired him, and Rollo clawed his way

over the crest of the hill until he rolled into the brambles. Among the thorns and weeds he could see the sun glinting off a golden object, and he reached a trembling claw toward the vision. It was a regal cup with twin handles, and rainbow-colored jewels encrusting its fat middle. Rollo had never seen anything so magnificent, and he doubted if anyone else in Bonespittle had either.

It has to be part of the Old Troll King's treasure, decided Rollo. With a trembling claw he reached for the blinding gold. In a flash, the vessel disappeared as his hand touched it.

Rollo cringed and scooted back a few feet, and the cup reappeared. 'What is this?' he asked in alarm. 'Who's there?'

'Nothing to fret about, my dear, just an illusion,' answered a soft voice that seemed to float on the gentle afternoon breeze. Somehow, it was a voice that sounded familiar.

'Do I know you?' asked the troll.

'My, yes, you know me,' answered the cheery voice from the golden cup. 'It's Melinda, the Enchantress Mother of the Bonny Woods. My distrust once got you captured, but then my hope freed you. Did Ludicra not tell you how I helped her?'

'Yes, she did!' answered the troll with relief. 'And you're here now, and you can help me get back to my comrades!'

'I'm afraid not,' said the elf sadly. 'I'm only really here for one thing. This is just a spirit stone that can look like another object, and I can behold through it. There are only a few spirit stones in the Great

Chasm, but they're useful for talking to Dwayne and his band.'

The shimmering cup turned into a gray stone of equal size, and Rollo blinked in amazement.

'Go ahead and pick it up,' said the voice of the Enchantress Mother. 'You can even take it with you, if you wish. But I warn you: Sometimes I'm unable to devote the concentration needed to use this stone. I won't always be there.'

'Can you do something to get me back to my friends?' asked Rollo. 'Time is running out. Stygius Rex is back, and he holds my father and Krunkle prisoner.'

'Why don't you fly?'

Rollo lowered his head glumly. 'I lost my power to fly.'

'You're just tired and confused . . . and worried,' answered the Enchantress. 'I know exactly how you feel. When you really need it, it will be back.'

The troll didn't think so, because it felt as if everything was going wrong. 'So can you help me get back to my friends?' he pleaded.

'I can look like a golden cup and talk to you,' answered the impatient voice. 'That's it. In fact, I have no idea *where* you are – it's a place I've never beheld except through this stone.'

'Well, a dragon brought me here,' said Rollo with frustration. 'We're at the very end of the Great Chasm, where there's supposed to be a glacier. Instead there's this swamp full of hot water.'

'Hmmm, a dragon bore you there,' said Melinda, sounding impressed. 'They say dragons like bright, shiny things.'

'They might,' answered Rollo, thinking of lustrous gold. 'Enchantress Mother, can the stone become that shiny vessel anytime you wish?'

'No,' she answered sadly. 'Not when I'm occupied elsewhere. I can make it pretty and leave it that way, but I would think someone would try to steal it.'

'Let's hope so,' answered Rollo as he gazed at the azure sky. 'Please let it be the trophy. If I can get rid of some things, I can fit it in my pack.'

'This is tiring for me,' said the Enchantress Mother, whose voice wavered as it came through the spirit stone. 'We will speak later. Protect this cup.'

With that, the river rock in his paws turned into a gleaming masterpiece of gold and jewels in the shape of a two-handled loving cup. The troll gasped at the wonder and almost dropped it. Then he hugged it to his chest and rose to his full height, glad that he finally had help, however limited. He was on high ground at last and could look around, and he saw great forests in the distance.

On the side of the chasm he had reached, it was the same scraggly desert as farther up the lava river. The troll could see the black mounds of steaming sludge where the lava met its match in the swamp. Perhaps there was a glacier farther north, beyond the verdant meadow, but Rollo couldn't tell from here.

A glance over his shoulder revealed nothing in the brilliant sky but mere wisps of clouds. Rollo emptied his pack, ate what dried worms he had left, and placed the shimmering goblet into his bag. The big troll shouldered his prize and trudged off into the desert that ran along the Bonespittle side of the rim.

NINE

No Honor Among Thieves

'Is that you, Clipper?' droned the voice in the dark stairwell. 'Where have you been for so long?'

'Oh, here and there, all over the Great Chasm,' answered the fairy. She tried using her magic to pierce the darkness that surrounded Stygius Rex, but it didn't help. 'I followed the trolls, the elves, everybody. Why are you sitting in such darkness, Master?'

'Why are you asking questions when you should be answering them?' replied the sorcerer. Clipper heard his clothing rustle, and he grunted. 'I don't like the light. This is better – my enemies can't find me.'

Clipper giggled. 'Surely you don't fear those silly trolls and ogres.'

'No!' thundered Stygius Rex. 'Not them ... other enemies. I sense them stirring.'

'Hmmm,' said the fairy. *Who could frighten Stygius Rex like this?* she wondered. *It must be the mysterious one who now commands me.*

The mage grumbled, 'Are you ever going to tell me about the treasure hunt?'

'The Bonespittle band are doing their best,' answered Clipper. 'The elves know where it is and have told the trolls. They even allowed the trolls and ogres to go ahead, and we must assume the loot is hard to get. Or else the elves would have gotten it.'

'Then why aren't you with them, helping them?' demanded Stygius Rex. 'Stay with them until you find out where it is!'

Clipper sniffed, sounding hurt. 'First you're mad that I waited so long to report, and now you're mad that I reported at all! Make up your mind!'

'Yes, yes . . . you've done well.' The mage shifted in the web of blackness that clung to the steps, and Clipper almost thought she saw him for a second. 'Now go back and watch them,' he ordered.

Now? thought the fairy with alarm. *Not now – I have to steal the dagger from you! What good is gold? The real prize is the black knife.*

'How are the prisoners?' Clipper asked innocently. 'Do you need me to make them sneeze?'

'They're sneezing just fine on their own,' snapped the mage. 'Be off with you, Clipper, and be wary out there. Perhaps I am worried for nothing. . . .' His voice trailed off.

Clipper was torn; she didn't know which way to go. All she knew was that she had to steal that knife . . .

again. Maybe she wouldn't even take it to her new friend
– maybe she would keep it for herself.

'Good-bye, Master,' she said as she flitted down the
stairs. The fairy flew some distance and crouched behind
one of the steps. From this new spot she didn't think
the sorcerer could see or hear her, but she could watch
him, waiting for a moment when he would let down
his guard. He had to sleep, didn't he?

After a while the fairy heard sniffling sounds, as if
the great sorcerer were crying. Minutes later he
muttered some words to himself, like a person talking
in his sleep.

'Come on, fellows, have some more slime stew!' she
heard him say. 'It's good for what ails you. Eat as much
as you want – you'll feel great!' Then he went back to
mumbling.

He's dreaming, thought Clipper. She was about to make
a dash for the serpent knife, even though Stygius Rex
was still bathed in magical darkness. She stopped when
she heard footsteps higher up in the tunnel.

The sorcerer stirred from his uneasy rest. 'Who goes
there?' he demanded. 'Is that you, Butcher?'

'Me Butcher,' snorted an ogre. 'Many big bugs up
here – *stinging* bugs. Could use a fireball.'

'Oh, you're such babies,' whined Stygius Rex. 'We've
got more to worry about than a few bugs. Use oil from
the lamps to burn them, and leave me alone . . . to
think.'

'Yes, Master. Sorry, Master.' The ogre's footsteps
shuffled away.

Clipper hunkered down behind the step, because the

sorcerer was again awake. But he was also weary and stressed, which meant he would probably fall back to sleep. The next time he did, she wouldn't hesitate to steal the knife – just like when she had stolen it from Rollo.

At the bottom of the chasm Ludicra led her hearty band, bashing her way through a morass of gnome-eating succulents. She didn't think it was possible, but the plants had multiplied as the party hiked upriver. Here it was an endless sea of carnivorous vines, blood-thirsty thorns, and itchy ivy. Even the lava flow seemed diminished by the huge growth, which sometimes towered over their heads.

As strong as she was, the young troll was exhausted from stomping and crawling over the thickets. She had a sturdy hide, but there were scratches all over her body, not to mention stickers and rashes.

With a grunt Ludicra swung her club at a vine that ducked out of the way. Her momentum carried her head over heels, and the troll landed in thick briars that tried to strangle her. Weevil and Crawfleece quickly dragged her out, and she staggered to her feet. She stood there for a few minutes, panting and swaying in the heat.

The troll glanced back to the path they had cleared, and she saw Captain Chomp and Gnat walking way behind them. At our slow pace, how can those two not keep up? Ludicra wanted to yell at the wounded ogre and little gnome to make them hurry, but she was too tired to yell.

Weevil slapped the troll on the back and said, 'Hey, don't feel bad. We're getting there.'

'I'm not sure we're still following the map,' said

Ludicra. She reached into her tattered vest and pulled out the flap of bark with smudged drawings all over it. 'Where are we on here?'

'Put that silly thing away,' said Crawfleece. 'We've got a sheer cliff on one side of us, and a river of fire on the other side. How can we go the wrong way?'

'Unless this is all a wicked joke the elves are playing on us,' added Weevil. 'They've set fake treasures and traps for us before. We have only their word that they know where this treasure is, and Dwayne might have drawn that map just to gain his freedom.'

'I don't think so,' insisted Ludicra, but she wasn't as certain as before. There was no sign of a path anywhere along this part of the canyon – it was all a sweaty tropical jungle. She looked worriedly at the map and said, 'We don't want to miss this pool of water.'

'It must be larger than these little geysers,' replied Crawfleece as she muscled ahead of Ludicra. 'It's my turn to take the lead.'

'No, wait,' said their leader. 'Captain Chomp and Gnat are falling farther behind us, and we all need to rest. Let's make our way to the cliff and try to find a clearing there.'

Weevil frowned. 'I don't like camping under the cliff. What if a rock falls from way up there?' The ogre pointed into the dismal reaches high above them. 'And we don't know where that stupid fairy may be lurking.'

'We'll use our shields for protection,' said Crawfleece. 'I agree with Ludicra – I'm tired of fighting these fiendish plants. Come along.'

With Crawfleece smashing a path, they trudged

through the steamy jungle until they reached the canyon wall. Piles of stones and rubble showed that rocks did sometimes fall from above. Weevil quickly erected a lean-to with her shield and crawled underneath it. Ludicra was just so relieved to get away from the snarl of plants that she collapsed to the ground. Crawfleece stood guard, waiting for Chomp and Gnat to catch up.

The wounded ogre and tired gnome staggered into camp a few minutes later, and they dropped where they stood. Rain pummeled them from above, but nobody minded it in this intense heat.

'Should we set up a guard?' asked Gnat.

Ludicra shrugged her beefy shoulders. 'Do you really think anyone will come around here to bother us? It's no wonder the elves don't journey this far – how can they get through these thickets? *We* can barely do it.'

'We're carving them a path,' Captain Chomp pointed out.

'Yes, we are,' said Ludicra thoughtfully. She looked back at the trail they had beaten through the snarled under-brush. 'We have to make sure we don't do their dirty work for them. We trolls are through working for others.'

Crawfleece laughed and swatted at a huge dragonfly. 'Are you saying that you don't trust doe-eyed Dwayne?'

'He does have pretty eyes, doesn't he?' asked Ludicra with a sigh. She quickly shook off the stray thought, because this was a life-or-death struggle. If they had the Old Troll King's treasure, they would have clout over Stygius Rex, Dwayne, and everyone else.

Ludicra surveyed the narrow path between the cliff and the spiny jungle, and she got an idea. 'If someone is following us, they would have to follow our path. So this would be a good place for a pit trap.'

Gnat sprung to his feet, clapping his talons with excitement. 'Dreadful idea . . . let's do it! And you know, as the captain and I took the rear we had the feeling we were being followed. A rustling in the weeds, a voice on the wind.'

'Keep your voices down,' warned Weevil, poking her head out from under her shield. 'We'll whisper until our plans are done, then we'll talk while we dig, to cover the noise.'

Captain Chomp snorted a laugh and said, 'This will pay those fools back for when we trailed them in the tunnel. Ludicra, just tell me when to talk loudly, and I will tell you some very funny ghoul stories.'

'The three of us will start digging,' said the troll, pointing to Crawfleece and Weevil.

Because they lived underground, digging was as natural as walking for the Bonespittlians. Captain Chomp told funny stories to cover up the noise and keep the spies at bay. With Gnat directing their efforts, the three brawny females scooped out an impressive pit. They cut thin branches to lay across the opening, and they covered it all with vines.

When they were done, they had a trap that was big enough to catch two or three unwary elves, and to slow down a larger party. Ludicra felt a bit guilty, but it was best to remind the elves who was going to control this treasure.

Refreshed from their efforts and excited about their trick, the band from Bonespittle found new strength. Soon they were hacking and lumbering through the brambles once again, with Crawfleece in the lead. Before they got a hundred feet, Ludicra heard two terrified screams behind them.

Everyone stopped, and they listened to some colorful elven cursing. Captain Chomp turned to the troll and laughed. 'It looks like your trap worked.'

'Well done!' crowed Gnat.

Everyone took a moment to appreciate the prank, but Ludicra forced her smile. She was worried that Dwayne might have fallen into the pit, but there was no time to think about the precious elf now.

'That should give us a good head start,' she said, puffing out her stomach. 'Keep on moving!'

With grunts and snarls the band of foul folk smashed their way through hungry succulents and barbed vines. A putrid mist hung over them, and the glow of the lava turned everything a fiery red.

Dwayne scowled with anger as he gazed down into the pit – to see his two miserable scouts. One elf had a broken leg, and the other a sprained ankle.

'We're sorry, my liege!' said one scout, hopping about. 'They took off suddenly from their camp, and we had to rush to catch up!'

The leader waved dismissively. 'Lower down a rope,' he told Fennel. 'Get them out.'

'Yes, sir,' answered the officer.

'Those despicable demons!' exclaimed Spree. 'How could they set this trap for us? After you *told* them where the treasure was.'

'I think they have long memories,' answered Dwayne.

'Or it could be they realized they were being followed.'

He could feel the eyes of every elf in his band looking at him accusingly. They hadn't argued with him before, but now they had to question his decision to be friendly to the trolls and ogres. The fey folk watched glumly as they fished their wounded comrades out of the hole.

'All right,' said the elven leader, 'we have to consider them to be the enemy. You wounded ones – wait here. The rest of us must go more slowly and with caution. Even if the trolls get the treasure, I don't see how they can get past us with it.'

'I hope not,' said Fennel. 'Or you will have to answer to all Elfdom.'

'They haven't found it yet,' declared Dwayne. The elven leader stomped ahead of the others but halted after a few steps. Cautiously Dwayne grabbed his unstrung bow and used it to prod the ground, looking for more traps. It was going to be a slow pace from there on, and the enemy had the lead.

Filbum had somehow thought that riding on horseback would be more pleasant than it was. Instead he banged along until his rump was so sore and stiff, he longed to walk. At his side were his two new partners, Sergeant Skull and Gouge. The ogres seemed more at ease in the saddle, but their horses labored beneath them. Filbum often had to slow down to keep from getting too far ahead of them.

On horseback crossing the Rawchill River was cold but easy, especially when Skull knew how to find the secret ford. Crossing the desert brought more pain and stiffness, and they rode day and night, walking the horses to rest them. It was day when they finally reached the Great Chasm, and even Skull was in awe. The grizzled warrior jumped off his horse, lowered his metal head, and stared into the abyss.

'How could someone fly across *that*?' he asked, waving at the monstrous gorge and the leafy green trees on the other side.

'Well, I've flown down it and up it, but never across,' said Filbum honestly. 'We should look for a path or some tracks.'

'I see them here!' called Gouge. The big ogre was bent over crushed desert shrubbery. 'Tracks lead that way, along the rim.'

'Back on horse,' ordered Sergeant Skull.

Once on their mounts the trio rode until they spotted two figures in the distance. As they approached, Filbum saw that two ogres guarded the hole Ludicra had made in the earth. So far no one had found the real entrance to the tunnel, but this one worked just as well.

The guards stiffened to attention as the three new arrivals rode up. Sergeant Skull didn't smile very often, but he tried to look friendly.

'Greetings, Drab! Possum!' he called to the ogres as he climbed off his horse. 'This duty goes well?'

The two ogre guards glanced uneasily at each other, and one of them snorted, 'Very well, Sergeant Skull. What do you need?'

'I need to go down there.' The ogre pointed a claw into the hole.

Drab shook his woolly head and huge tusks. 'The

master told us not to let anyone go down. He said, "not anyone."'

'I'm not "anyone"!' roared Skull. The ogre jumped into the guard's face and met him tusk to tusk as the metal bowl on his head gleamed in the sun. 'Drab, you served *me* until I sent you here. I have urgent message for Stygius Rex. We go tell him, and you wait here with horses.'

'We can have the horses?' asked the other guard in rapture, and Drab glared at him.

'The master says no one down there,' insisted the big ogre. 'That includes Sergeant Skull. Big secret.'

'Oh, you mean the treasure,' Skull said with a chuckle. When surprise flashed across their faces, the grizzled ogre laughed even harder. 'Oh, I know all about the treasure. What you think this message is about? Now step aside.'

'But our orders!' said Possum, stiffening his spine and not moving from the hole.

Sergeant Skull came snout to snout with the younger ogre. 'You want to take me on, Junior? I teach you everything you know, and I still know more than you.'

Gouge jumped off his horse and handed the reins to Filbum. The brute stepped forward, waving his club. 'You stupid ogres get out of our way! This is Sergeant Skull you talk to – when it comes to ogres, *he's* your master!'

Filbum could see the ogres thinking, which was difficult for them. He hoped Drab and Possum would be sensible, but fear of Stygius Rex was strong. Possum flinched and went for his club, but Skull swung a leg and caught his foe from behind. With a shove Skull tripped the big ogre and sent him tumbling into the hole. Gouge and Drab exchanged a couple of blows with their clubs, while Filbum held on to the horses and tried to calm them.

When Skull smashed Drab from behind, the battle was over and the two guards were knocked out. 'They can take care of horses when they wake up,' said Skull. 'Get the packs and torches.'

While they pulled supplies off the horses, Filbum scanned the parched horizon, looking for a force of trolls in the desert. But that was pointless because it would take Vulgalia some nights to spread the word, if she even did. They had come to the chasm the swiftest way on horseback, and nobody on foot was going to catch them. Nothing was going to stop Filbum from going into the ground with these two greedy ogres – his new partners in treasure hunting.

Sergeant Skull lit a torch and tossed a backpack to Filbum, then pointed into the hole. 'After you, troll.'

'Why, thank you,' Filbum said with a gulp. 'Uh, what are we going to do when we meet Stygius Rex?'

Skull scratched his metal noggin and asked, 'You know where the treasure is, right?'

'Yes,' Filbum lied.

'Then why do we need a sorcerer?' Skull looked at Gouge, and the two ogres laughed.

Filbum forced a laugh too. Somehow, whenever he lied, things got worse. But at least he was leading some kind of force against Stygius Rex. For the second time in his life Filbum jumped into the dark passageway that led to the bottom of the Great Chasm.

TEN

Landmark

Another short day with a few minutes of sunlight graced the bottom of the Great Chasm. Just as quickly the light crept up the side of the cliff and was gone. This plunged Ludicra and her companions back into a red-hued netherworld of mists and fire.

As they hacked their way through the weeds Ludicra feared that the deadline given them by Stygius Rex was almost over. He had said two days, but she tried not to worry about it. Time passed slowly in this ageless gorge, where no one could see stars, moon, or sun. Even so, they got into a rhythm with their slashing through the thickets, and their pace improved.

Whenever they rested, they took the time to set a small trap for their elven friends. Sometimes it was a rope snare, a trip wire, or another pit. Ludicra doubted whether their tricks wreaked much damage, but they were enough to slow them down. She felt guilty, but she knew the elves would do the same to them.

If there really was treasure in this fiery gorge, Ludicra didn't want elves breathing down their necks as they tried to get it. She would be glad to give them some of the loot, but only after they had defeated Stygius Rex . . . again. There was no way any of them could find peace or happiness with the greedy sorcerer around.

Ludicra also worried about the mysterious stranger she had met – the one who had saved her life when she was falling into the lava. He seemed to be more interested in the cursed knife than the treasure, but he had power. Even in the heat Ludicra shivered to think about the cloaked stranger, and she didn't want to meet him again.

Through the constant twilight they hacked deeper into a snarl of plants that lashed and snapped at them. Ludicra could barely see the canyon wall, and it seemed to be getting farther away. They traveled no closer to the burning ooze than they had to, so maybe the canyon was getting wider. The ashes, fog, and rancid smells were also stronger, and burning embers swirled in the air.

Ludicra gazed upward into the darkness above them and longed to be on the rim – or at least in fresh air. The constant stench was making her sick and depressed, and none of them were talking to one another anymore. After all this heat and stink, the troll would even welcome a bath in the Rawchill River.

As she gazed upward a shadow seemed to blacken out the mist, and she ducked.

'Ludicra, what is it?' asked Crawfleece in alarm. 'Elven arrows?'

The troll scanned the sky, but she couldn't see anything now. 'A bird, I think. *Something* flew overhead.'

'The birds are our friends, aren't they?' asked Captain Chomp, rubbing the bump on his head.

'Some of them do the sorcerer's bidding,' answered Gnat. He glanced at Ludicra and added, 'Or they follow the wicked fairy.'

Chomp groaned. 'I get so confused.'

On the path ahead of them Weevil stopped her bashing and stood hunched over, panting. 'Come on, why did you stop to talk? Are we making camp here?'

Everyone looked with hope at Ludicra, as if that wouldn't be a bad idea. But the stout troll shook her head. 'Keep moving – I think we're close to something. I'll take the lead if you're tired, Weevil.'

'No,' wheezed the wiry ogre, 'what gave you that idea?' At once she dove back into the morass of vines and weeds, hacking and slashing a path.

They traveled for another large chunk of a day, or night, or whatever it was above them. Ludicra was in the lead, bashing down the weeds, when she found herself plowing uphill. The plants thinned out and were no longer as dangerous as before, so she climbed the hill to see what she could see. Ludicra heard her comrades scrambling to catch up with her.

When she reached the top, the troll stopped and stared at something amazing. In the distance of the canyon the river of fire seemed to rise straight up into the air, where it joined a huge plume of flame. Ludicra

was alarmed until she realized how far away this
startling sight had to be.

'What is it?' breathed Crawfleece, looming behind her.

'I'm not sure,' answered Ludicra, 'but I think it's the
source of the lava – the volcano.'

'Dangle me,' replied Crawfleece. 'That's a big fire
mountain.'

'Good thing it's far away,' said Weevil as she joined
her comrades. 'What else is up there?'

The volcano was so amazing, Ludicra forgot to look
around. When she did, she realized they were on a rocky
plateau with fewer plants. The lava was a safe distance
away, but they were surrounded by geysers that
squirted steam into the sky. Some of this water
condensed and flowed into small pools, which shimmered red like blood.

Ludicra didn't think any of these puddles were the
large pool on Dwayne's map, but this was the first sign
of standing water. Maybe there really was a large pool
up ahead.

Captain Chomp and Gnat caught up with them, and
the ogre and the gnome stood in awe for several seconds.

'We must turn back,' squeaked Gnat. 'This doesn't
look like a safe place.' The squat gnome turned on his
heel and tried to run.

'No turning back!' roared Chomp, grabbing his small
companion. 'We're getting close – I can smell the jewels
and pearls.'

'Chomp, you wouldn't know a pearl if you ate an
oyster bed,' scoffed Weevil. 'I say we should scout ahead
before we march into trouble.'

Crawfleece stepped away from the group. 'At least we don't have to hack and chop our way. I'll go ahead.'

'I'll go with you,' offered Ludicra. She fought the temptation to take out Dwayne's map and look at it, because she had already done so a hundred times. Each time she did, it reminded everyone how much she trusted the cute elf. Besides, she knew the map didn't show this plateau or the volcano, which could mean they were on a wild bat chase.

'Captain Chomp and Gnat should rest,' ordered Ludicra. 'Weevil, you stay and guard them.'

'Come on,' said Crawfleece, striding ahead.

The trolls moved quickly and didn't pause at all, because the flat rock was hot on their feet. They had to duck scalding geysers, which shot steam at them without warning, while they jumped over boiling puddles. Glancing to her right, Ludicra could see the lava churning just below the edge of the rock – it felt good to be above the flames.

After a long march dodging hot showers and swirling sparks, Ludicra and Crawfleece started downhill. There were rivulets of steaming water running in the crevices, and it had to be flowing toward a central pool. Ludicra could feel slime under her bare feet, and it reminded her of home.

A moment later she gasped because she almost stepped into their destination – a large pool of flaming red liquid. It was only that color because of the reflection from the lava, but the smooth span of water still entranced her.

'The pool!' breathed Ludicra. 'This has to be the landmark from the map.' Her eyes rose from the shimmering water to scan the jagged cliffs above the pool. The troll searched for other landmarks – the narrow ledge and the treasure – but all she saw was eerie fog and shifting shadows.

'We're going to need more light,' said Crawfleece, 'so we can see what we're doing.'

'Go back and get the others,' whispered Ludicra. 'I'll guard this place.'

Crawfleece shook her shaggy head. 'Are you sure you want me to leave you here alone?'

'Just bring them,' answered Ludicra. 'I'll look for a way up.'

With a snort Crawfleece hurried away, dodging a geyser that tried to douse her. In a moment Ludicra was alone on the plateau, surrounded by rock, water, and fire. The troll was suddenly very thirsty, and she wondered whether the liquid was fit to drink. She got down on her knees and crawled forward, reaching a point on the slimy bank where she could reach the water.

Gingerly Ludicra dipped her claw into the pool, and the reflection broke into a million shimmering red worms. The water was warm to the touch, not scalding as the fresh puddles were, and she lifted her wet digits to her snout and sniffed. The troll's senses had been blasted by all the foul gases in the Great Chasm, but the water smelled clean to her.

For a long time Ludicra slurped from the pool, quenching a thirst that ran very deep. As she finished drinking she heard a slight chirping noise beside her, and she turned to see a remarkable creature. It had leathery wings, a long beak with sharp teeth, a slender neck, and bronze-colored scales. The animal seemed to stand on three legs like a tripod, and it was about her size, at least when both of them were in a crouch.

The slender neck twisted about, and beady eyes and sharp fangs loomed in her face. With a gulp Ludicra realized that this winged creature might be hungry, too, and perhaps trolls were on the menu. Now she wished she hadn't sent Crawfleece away. The monster had small feet and claws; it rested on its bent wings and long tail, which formed the tripod.

The being opened its mouth and cooed and chirped, as if glad to see her. *This is just a chance meeting at the water hole,* Ludicra told herself as she slowly backed away.

The troll didn't get very far, because she bumped into what felt like a dagger at her back. She whirled around to see another creature identical to the first, except this one had bluish scales. The two of them could pick her apart in no time, and Ludicra reached for her club.

Before she had to fight the flying beasts, a shriek sounded high up the side of the cliff. Both creatures craned their necks to listen. When the horrible cry came again, the pair unfurled their massive wings and began to flap. The wind from their wings nearly knocked Ludicra into the water, but she held her ground on the slippery slope.

The flyers hopped along the rock, flapping their immense wings until they finally took off. They circled gracefully in the fog and headed up the side of the cliff. It was a good thing that Ludicra was watching the sky, because a monstrous shape came streaking toward her.

The troll barely had time to flop to her belly before the winged behemoth raked her back with sharp talons.

'Yaaaah!' cried Ludicra in pain. She quickly rolled into the water, and the warm liquid brought some relief to her fresh wounds.

Ludicra lifted her club, ready to fight back, but the black shape rose swiftly into the air. It squawked loudly, and two calls answered from a distance. Sopping wet, Ludicra staggered to her feet and watched as the three beasts vanished into the yellow mist clinging to the side of the cliff.

If the treasure is up there somewhere, she thought, *no wonder nobody has been able to get it.*

In the dark tunnel Filbum struggled to catch his breath. The two ogres leaped down the stairs ahead of him, trying to beat each other to the bottom of the Great Chasm. They made much better time than Ludicra's party had. Of course, the ogres didn't have to fight their way through wicked elves, giant snails, armies of millipedes, serpents, and traps the way the other group had. This trip it was as if the passageway had been swept clean of trouble.

The troll had seen the charred remains of fireballs where Stygius Rex had cleared some local wildlife out of the way. All of the missing steps were obvious and the traps had been sprung and were easy to avoid. Filbum felt nostalgic for the way the tunnel had been a week ago – wild and untouched, like a carefree wilderness. Now the once-secret passageway was showing signs of heavy traffic.

Filbum took a ragged breath and hurried after his

companions. He had his own torch, so he wasn't in the dark; still, he wanted to know what his insane partners were doing. Although he liked it down here, he didn't want to be left alone in the spooky stairwell with a wicked mage and a demented fairy on the loose. So the troll skipped down the stairs like his companions. In his haste Filbum banged against the wall and nearly dropped his torch.

'Be still!' a voice hissed in the darkness. 'Put your light out.'

Filbum lowered his torch and caught a glimpse of Sergeant Skull's gleaming cranium. The ogre's beady eyes stared at the young troll, and he quickly stubbed out his torch in a dusty corner. 'What is it?'

'We very near to them,' whispered the old warrior. 'We smell their fires and their gopher grease. Air rise up – we smell *them*, they no smell *us*.'

That was good for them, because he could clearly smell Sergeant Skull – and he was rank. The troll coughed and asked, 'Where is Gouge?'

Skull snorted. 'Gouge go ahead to check how close . . . and how many. How many ogres you see before?'

'Two, maybe three,' answered Filbum. 'That's all I remember.'

'Me think he took four ogres with him,' said Skull with a toothsome grin. 'That make two above and two below. Good! Ogres we can take by surprise, and they may not fight us. But Stygius Rex is tough.'

'You're telling me,' whispered Filbum. 'We need a plan for the Rexster.'

Filbum scratched the stubble on his chin, while

Sergeant Skull scratched the metal dome on his head. 'Did I tell you?' grumbled the troll. 'He rolled a big boulder down on us.'

Skull's rheumy eyes widened. 'You got a big boulder?'

'No.'

'Me neither.' The ogre frowned in troubled thought.

'That's a bad idea, anyway,' muttered Filbum. He was thinking of the hostages, because that was a good way to get them killed. He hadn't told the ogres about Krunkle and Nulneck, and he wanted to keep it that way . . . for now.

'Would a flying troll do the trick?' asked Filbum.

Skull clicked his slimy tusks. 'Do we have one of those?'

'Yes . . . I think.'

'Master will think it is Rollo,' said the warrior with a chuckle. 'If it is dark, and he see ogres, he will think they are *his* ogres.'

'So you take care of his ogres, switch places with them, and act like you're chasing me.' Filbum gulped because this plan might also get him bashed or captured, especially if Skull and Gouge decided to switch and go back to Stygius Rex.

'You know, if he gets the treasure,' whispered the troll, 'he won't give you any.'

Sergeant Skull snorted. 'If Master even know we know about it, he probably gut us like a coconut.'

'There is that possibility,' said Filbum with a shiver.

A few seconds later they heard shuffling sounds on the stairs below them, and Skull hefted his massive club. He squeaked like a bat and was answered by a similar bat squeak beneath him. They waited in darkness until Gouge bumped into them.

'Report,' ordered Skull.

'A couple of ours,' replied the brawny ogre. 'Unless my nose is bad, also two trolls.'

'Trolls?' Skull peered angrily at Filbum. 'Why trolls with Stygius Rex?'

'They're prisoners,' admitted the youth. 'It's Krunkle, the master bridge builder, and Nulneck, Rollo's father. I don't know why, but he wants to keep them close at hand.'

'They know about treasure?' asked Sergeant Skull suspiciously.

'No,' answered Filbum quickly. 'If we untie them, I'm sure they'll just run up to the top.'

'Hmmm,' said Skull. 'Where is sorcerer?'

Gouge grunted. 'Must be farther down . . . or gone. What do we do?'

'We take out ogres and untie trolls,' answered the sergeant. 'Troll here fly toward Stygius Rex, cause great ruckus, and we chase him. While Rexster is distracted, we bash him.'

'That sounds brilliant,' said Gouge.

'My idea,' lied Skull. 'We surprise the master, eh?'

'Stop talking and go!' squeaked Filbum. He wanted to do it while he still had his courage.

Shushing each other, the ogres slipped down the darkened stairs, while Filbum padded behind them. Soon he could smell the cook fire and gopher grease, and it made him hungry. A bit later he saw a pool of light on a lower step, and he heard some guttural ogre voices. They didn't seem too concerned about an attack coming from the top.

Skull and Gouge didn't waste any time as they leaped down the stairs and bashed their fellow ogres. Luckily the captive trolls were tied up and lying on the steps, so they escaped the worst of the melee. With surprise on their side it was a short battle, and Filbum was soon cutting the ropes off Krunkle and Nulneck.

'Run to the top,' he told the prisoners. 'Don't stop, don't look back . . . just go.'

'Thank you,' rasped Nulneck as he staggered to his feet. Filbum gave them a burning log to use as a torch, and the two elder trolls scurried up the steps.

'What is going on up there?' growled a voice from below. It was Stygius Rex!

Sergeant Skull grabbed Filbum by the scruff of his neck and almost threw him down the stairs. The troll tried to fly, but he tripped and went rolling down the stairs head over heels.

'The Troll King!' cried Sergeant Skull as he and Gouge thundered down the steps behind him.

When Filbum, with a huge knot on his head, finally came to rest on the stairs, he could see nothing. It was blacker than black down there – blacker than the rest of the tunnel, blacker than the sorcerer's heart. But the frightened troll could hear breathing nearby, and it turned into a wheezing laugh.

'This is not Rollo,' said Stygius Rex with disdain. 'A fireball will tell me who you are.'

The dingy stairwell was suddenly lit up as if it were broad daylight, and a blob of fire streaked toward Filbum's head!

ELEVEN

Seeds of Destruction

For hours, maybe days, Clipper had been crouching on a lower step of the cramped stairwell, waiting for an opportunity to steal the black serpent knife. The demented fairy knew she couldn't make a direct attack on Stygius Rex, because the sorcerer was too wily. She had to wait until a special moment presented itself.

This was the moment.

Clipper heard a crush of voices, lots of noise, something big tumbling down the stairs, and the mage's voice. That was followed by an explosion of light that almost blinded her. Clipper flew up the steps before she even thought about what she was doing. Moving like a glint of light, the sprite spotted Stygius Rex with a fireball in his hand, about to kill some poor troll.

Once again the fleet fairy didn't think too much. She zoomed to the mage's waist and grabbed his cloak with one hand and the hilt of the black knife with the other. When she performed this action, it startled him – just as he unleashed his fireball. The flaming missile went awry and veered up the steps, where it blasted two surprised ogres.

'You rotten little pixie!' yelled the mage as he steadied himself against the wall. She tried to draw the precious dagger from the sheath, and it came out a few inches. But Stygius Rex snarled and swiped a claw at her, knocking her hands away from the prize. The fairy screeched like a wounded banshee, thinking all was lost.

It would have been lost had not the troll acted when he did. The fearsome brute leaped up and smashed Stygius Rex in the snout with his massive fist. Noxious pink blood splattered Clipper, but she didn't care as she dove for the knife. With a howl of shock the sorcerer swung his arms to keep his balance just as Clipper reached the hilt and got a firm grip. Then the troll hit him again on his warty chin.

With a wail the wounded mage dropped backward, letting Clipper draw the knife as the sheath fell away. He rolled down the stairs while Clipper clutched the dark weapon to her pale body. She felt power and evil surging through her tiny body.

'You're mine now,' whispered the fairy.

For the first time the troll became aware of her. He tried to spear her wing with a talon and just missed, and she darted away from him. On her flight down the stairwell, the fairy passed the crumpled body of Stygius Rex, and he moaned to her.

'Don't take the knife!' he begged. 'You'll regret it! I beg you, Clipper, don't—'

He mumbled something else, but Clipper ignored him. The ecstatic fairy gripped her prize and kept flying toward the faint red light at the bottom of the long passageway.

Filbum shook his fist because it hurt like crazy after punching Stygius Rex twice. That sorcerer had a hard head. The troll smelled something funny and looked back to see the two ogres, Skull and Gouge, trying to put out the flames on their pelts. The sorcerer's fireball had caught them squarely, and they were both still in shock and on fire.

This might be a good time to run for it, thought Filbum. So he did.

'Hey!' shouted Sergeant Skull. 'Where you going?'

Filbum didn't feel a great need to stop and chat with the ogres — he just barreled down the stairs. He was thankful there was enough light from the fire to see Stygius Rex lying in a heap on the stairs. The sorcerer barely looked up as the troll jumped over him. For a brief moment, Filbum almost felt sorry for the broken wizard, who had lost his most prized possession.

As he ran Filbum kept an eye open for the treacherous fairy, but he didn't see Clipper anywhere. She was probably happy just to run for it, as he was doing. Both of them had been successful — he had freed the hostages, and she had stolen the cursed knife. The only thing left to do was escape.

When he spotted a faint glow of light at the bottom,

Filbum increased his pace. He even tried to fly, and he skimmed over a few steps. A blast of heat hit the troll as he ran out of the tunnel into the foggy, smelly gulch with its bubbling river of fire. He was hoping to find his comrades waiting for him, but there was no one around the exit.

Filbum heard angry ogre howls behind him, and he looked around for some tracks in the grimy sand. When he found them going both ways, he just picked a direction and ran. He had no doubt that Skull and Gouge would be right on his heels, because ogres hated to get cheated out of treasure, especially by trolls.

Rollo trudged along the rim of the Great Chasm, trying to keep his eyes open and his feet moving. Clutched in his hands was the golden, two-handled loving cup, which was really a spirit stone. He had walked all day and all night, trying to reach the passageway to the bottom of the chasm, but he realized it was a tremendous distance. Even if he could still fly, he'd be lucky to get there in a week.

A new day was just starting, and the sun would soon rise over the scraggly trees on the other side. So Rollo glanced over his shoulder to look for a flying beast in the gray sky. He didn't think the dragon had passed him during the night, although that was possible. Rollo thought he would *feel* the dragon's presence, or at least hear those mighty wings beating against the wind.

The troll was lonely and worried, and he wanted to use the spirit stone to talk to the Enchantress Mother.

But he knew this was sleep time for the elves, and Melinda had been weary the night before. He dug for grubs and ate some bitter berries, and after breakfast he kept marching.

The sun came up, and the golden warmth hit his weary body, making him feel better. The troll looked over his shoulder, but the sky was still empty except for a few salmon-colored clouds. In his imagination Rollo could see his parents, Ludicra, Crawfleece, Filbum, the Dismal Swamp, trolls, and ogres. They were all smiling and happy – it was a grand occasion!

He didn't know where this vision came from, but he was content to hold it to his heart as he trudged along the rim of the vast canyon.

Clipper wanted to keep the black serpent knife for herself, but what good did a cursed knife do for a fairy? *I can barely carry it without dropping it, and I don't have a stack of bodies that need to be brought back to life.* Still, there was something soothing about possessing a depraved dagger with dreadful powers.

As she flew through the fetid fumes of the canyon, the fairy heard a voice in her head: *Come this way – to the right, across the river.*

'Why should I bring the knife to *you*?' she asked aloud. 'What did you ever do for me? This is *my* nasty knife!'

No, I forged it, said the voice, *just like I forged this entire canyon. I should have known Stygius Rex would kill all of us for it.*

'All of you?' asked the fairy, coming to a stop and fluttering. 'Who *are* you? Are you a ghost?'

Come and see, said the voice in her head. *I am just across the lava on the red sand beach.*

Clipper felt a tug on the knife, as if it were being summoned to the other side of the river too. 'It's mine,' she declared, 'so why can't I give it to whomever I want?'

Clutching the dagger tightly with both arms, the fairy zoomed across the blazing flow. She saw him in the yellow mist – the same small, hooded figure she had met when having fun with the trolls. She was beginning to like trolls; they made such comical buffoons and useful allies.

He was standing on red pumice sand, waiting for her as if he knew she would come. Clipper fluttered to a stop just out of his reach and and tried to stare under his hood. All she saw was a wizened chin, a pug nose, and intense black eyes.

'Time for answers,' she said. 'Are you an elf? A wraith? What do you mean, Stygius Rex killed all of you?'

'He didn't kill all of us, but he tried,' answered the figure. 'I am Batmole, formerly a sorcerer in Bonespittle.'

'I've heard of you,' said Clipper with admiration. 'You made the Great Chasm. Well done!'

'To be technical, I made an earthquake, a volcano, and a flood,' answered Batmole. 'I'm an elemental sorcerer, you see. But it took a lot out of me, and I slept for a year afterward in a hidden place. During that time the Troll King's treasure was lost, and the sorcerers took over Bonespittle. Before I awoke, Stygius Rex poisoned all of them, and I was presumed dead.'

The mage chuckled. 'Of course, you've also been dead, Clipper, so you know it's not entirely bad. You don't have much responsibility when you're dead. When I awoke, I was still weakened, so I didn't seek revenge on Stygius Rex. For one thing, if I defeated him, *I* would have to rule Bonespittle. That post was of no interest to me.'

He coughed lightly from a wisp of noxious fog. 'For a thousand years I retired to my retreat at the end of the chasm to do experiments and regain my powers. I didn't think I would become involved in worldly affairs again, until these two trolls fell into my clutches.'

'Aren't trolls funny!' said Clipper with amusement.

'They eat a lot,' answered Batmole with a scowl. 'When they started talking about the serpent knife and the Troll Treasure, that got my interest. So here we are. I need that toy you hold in your hands – to weaken Stygius Rex.'

'Oh, this?' Clipper lifted the precious dagger and chuckled. 'But it's mine, Batworm!'

'Batmole,' he corrected her. The knife suddenly grew very heavy in her arms, and she almost dropped it. Flapping her wings frantically, the fairy tried to rise into the air, but the weapon quadrupled in weight. It threatened to drag her to the ground! The fairy couldn't fly in reverse, because she was right over the lava bed. The mage had planned it that way when he'd chosen to meet her there.

Batmole suddenly lunged for the dagger, and Clipper had just enough strength left to fly over the lava, despite her better judgment. That was when the steam and fog and weight of the weapon made her lose her grip, and the dagger slipped out of her arms. 'No!' she cried.

'No!' cried Batmole.

Clipper reached for it, while the mage held out his hand and cast a spell, suspending the dagger in midair . . . inches above the flaming lava. Fearful he would get the prize, the fairy cast a spell of her own. Batmole gave a loud sneeze, snapping his head down.

When he did so, the black serpent knife fell into the flames and was consumed by molten magma. In seconds it became a dark, oily ooze on top of the flaming surge. Both the mage and the fairy began to weep in unison, and Clipper was so distraught, she zoomed straight up into the air. She couldn't remember anything that had happened, only that something rare had been lost forever.

Filbum crashed through the brambles and thorn bushes until his hide was coated with stickers and nettles. Hungry vines lashed at him, but he paid them no attention – he was certain that brawny ogres were chasing him. He could hear noises behind, but that was probably his own labored breathing or his stomach growling.

The weary troll staggered to the side of a boulder and leaned against it, glad to find a place that wasn't full of thorns. He listened carefully to find out if the ogres really were right behind him, and all he heard was some muffled weeping. Filbum ducked down, certain there was someone above him on the boulder. He listened again, and the weeping turned into heartfelt sobs.

Sobbing ogres were rather unusual, and he didn't see how Skull and Gouge could have gotten ahead of him. So Filbum stepped away from the rock and craned his neck to see the top of it. There he saw a hunched figure dressed in black, weeping into his hands.

Stygius Rex.

Filbum ducked again, certain that a fireball was about to kill him, but the slender sorcerer just waved. 'Fear not, little troll, I won't hurt you.'

The troll peered between the talons he had over his eyes. 'Are you sure you won't hurt me?'

'Absolutely c-certain,' stammered the mage through his sobs. 'I'm never going to hurt anyone again, and I'm sorry if I mistreated you before.'

Filbum rose to his feet and asked, 'You are Stygius Rex, aren't you?'

'I'm ashamed to admit it,' said the sorcerer, 'but I am he. And you're the one who hit me in the tunnel.'

Filbum laughed nervously. 'Yeah, but don't take that personally.'

The mage nodded with understanding. 'Of course not. You just wanted to free your friends. I quite understand.'

'Do you feel all right?' asked Filbum.

The elder gave him a crinkled smile. 'No, I feel rather poorly. Thank you for asking.' He shook his head as if trying to remember something important he had forgotten. 'I feel terrible remorse for all those bad things I did to you and your friends. It's odd, because I never felt this way before. I hope you can forgive me.'

'You don't want to take over Bonespittle and the Bonny Woods, and make us all slaves?'

'Heavens, no!' The cadaverous sorcerer looked shocked at the very idea. 'Didn't the citizens of Bonespittle already choose a leader? They want Rollo, not me. And we must help Rollo get the treasure – it belongs to the trolls.'

'You really don't feel well, do you?' asked Filbum. 'Or is this some kind of trick?'

'Some kind of trick?' echoed Stygius Rex. The skinny sorcerer broke into tears. 'That is such a hurtful thing to say to me! Believe me, I want only to help you. Do you want proof?'

'Proof would be nice,' answered Filbum.

'Well, I could stop those two ogres who are about to burst from the bushes and club you to death.'

'That would be good!' exclaimed Filbum. He whirled around to see Sergeant Skull and Gouge come charging out of the thickets, clubs raised and roaring with anger.

Stygius Rex calmly tossed a fireball, and the flaming missile streaked toward the startled ogres. Skull and Gouge were already singed from before, and their eyes widened in their blackened faces. The fireball exploded all around them, setting every plant in a ten-foot radius on fire. Howling in pain, their fur aflame, the two ogres hopped away.

'Hmmm,' said Stygius Rex, 'I never had a fireball go so straight before. That is interesting.'

Filbum knew he shouldn't believe the wily old mage, but he had been around goodness lately and had come to recognize it. This was not the Stygius Rex who had trollnapped half the village to build his bridge. This was a changed mage.

'How did you get here ahead of me?' asked Filbum, strolling back toward the boulder.

'I can still fly,' answered the sorcerer. 'I feel very sad over the awful things I've done, but I don't feel fear anymore. I am free to start over. Do you want to join your companions?'

'Yes, yes!' answered Filbum, jumping excitedly. 'Do you know where they are?'

Stygius Rex nodded and pointed across the river of lava. 'On that side, near the treasure. You can still fly, can't you?'

Filbum gulped. 'I *think* so.'

'Then come on.' The sorcerer rose to his stately height and leaped off the boulder; he floated down and landed gracefully in front of Filbum. The wizard smiled warmly, and even the hairy warts on his face looked friendly. 'You will have to trust me now. I'm part troll, did you know that?'

'No,' answered Filbum in amazement. Even as a cruel joke he didn't think Stygius Rex would ever admit to such a thing.

'It's true,' said Stygius Rex wistfully. 'We might even be related. What's your name?'

'Filbum.'

He shook his head. 'I don't remember any Filbums in my family, but you can still trust me. I think it's a good idea to get across the lava, because Sergeant Skull is going to come back as soon as he puts out the fire on his back.'

'Yes, let's go,' replied the troll, with a worried look behind him.

Like a father the elder put his arm around the troll's shoulders. 'Fear not, Filbum, your uncle Stygius Rex is here to protect you.'

Filbum tried not to cringe at the sickly touch and sweet smile of the old mage. He was almost *too* nice.

Before Filbum could think any more about it, his feet lifted from the ground, and the two of them began to float over the hot bubbling lava.

'Rollo,' said the golden cup in the troll's arms. 'Where are we?'

'Hello, Melinda,' answered Rollo. 'We're still walking.'

He felt funny talking to a golden cup, and he had to remind himself that the Enchantress Mother was using the vessel to communicate. He stopped to wipe the sweat off his hairy brow. The sun was rising high overhead, and its light would soon reach the bottom regions of the canyon. It was already hot along the rim, where he had been walking day and night.

Rollo vowed, 'I don't know if we'll ever get back to Bonespittle, but we're going to try.'

'Something strange is happening in the chasm,' came the voice of the elder elf. 'I feel it. Do you know what has become of the serpent knife?'

Rollo shrugged. 'Last I saw, Stygius Rex had it, and he didn't want to give it up.'

'But he has given it up,' replied Melinda. 'Or something has happened to it. I have a strong sense of this.'

Rollo shivered because that black dagger was bad news. He thought about the weird hermit in the stone hut – the one who had trapped them. With sorrow he thought about his friend Filbum, who had perhaps turned into a wisp of smoke. It didn't seem likely that any of them would get out of the Great Chasm alive.

The cup seemed to be snoring in his hands, and he

figured Melinda had dropped off to sleep. The elf was elderly and under siege at home, and he knew he shouldn't expect too much from her. That was when he heard a distant roar in the sky.

The troll whirled around to see monstrous wings flapping in the glare of the noonday sun. The beast was headed in his general direction, and Rollo lifted the cup above his head to catch the sun's blazing rays. The glare blinded him, and he hoped the beacon was shining to the skies as well.

The dragon was still some distance away, and he angled the trophy to catch its attention. Standing on the rim, surrounded by desert, Rollo figured the monster would get a clear look. When the dragon suddenly veered toward him, Rollo held his breath – he knew he was in for another exciting flight. He gripped one handle and held the other handle aloft.

Within seconds leathery wings, a hawkish head, bronze scales, and monstrous claws filled the sky. The troll was almost knocked over by the wind from the dragon's wings, and he feared the mammoth jaws would scoop him up.

The creature had to slow down to snag the cup, but it still almost ripped the prize from Rollo's hands. Barely holding on to the handle, the troll shot into the sky like a geyser. Rollo got a better grip on the cup and tried to make himself comfortable as he hung from the dragon's claws. He was headed in the right direction, so there was a chance he might get home – back to Ludicra, his family and friends, and his enemies.

There was just one problem: If he couldn't fly, how was he going to get off this ride?

TWELVE

Rags To Riches

Weevil slid carefully down the side of the cliff on a rope, after planting the last piton higher up. Ludicra held the rope for the ogre, and she looked nervously around the bottom of the gorge. Sunlight was starting to flow down the far cliff, like paint running on a wall.

Gnat was at the top of the rope, waiting to set another piton to hold their lines. Crawfleece and Captain Chomp stood guard, with clubs ready, watching out for elves. The band intended to climb the sheer cliff – to find the narrow ledge on the map. Dwayne had said they could see the treasure from that spot, which was good because they sure couldn't see it from down here.

This process had taken longer than expected, and Ludicra was certain the elves must have caught up with them. She could sense them lurking in the darkness, watching. The troll wanted to make their climb before daylight flooded the canyon and made them easy targets for poisoned arrows. She also remembered the strange flying creatures she had met at the pool. 'Hurry!' she whispered to Weevil.

The ogre dropped the last few feet and nearly landed on top of Ludicra. 'Is that fast enough?' she asked.

The troll shook off the blow and stepped back. 'Did you see it – the ledge?'

'Yes, Gnat is almost there,' answered Weevil in a low voice. 'That rock is hard – it's difficult to pound in the pitons. But they held my weight.'

Captain Chomp glanced worriedly at the slim ropes hanging against the sheer cliff. 'Do we *all* have to climb up there?' he asked. 'Can't some of us stand guard here on the ground?'

'The elves might overwhelm you,' answered Ludicra.

'We'll get defensive positions – high ground,' answered the ogre. 'We can use the pool as a buffer zone. Ludicra, how are you going to get down if the elves decide to pin you up there with arrows? We don't even know there *is* treasure here.'

Ludicra wanted to defend the map drawn by Dwayne, but she didn't have any proof it was true. She only knew that Dwayne and his comrades were out there skulking in the bushes and the fog, waiting to claim the treasure for themselves.

'You're right,' she told Chomp. 'You and Crawfleece stay down here and use the pool for cover.'

Suddenly the rope began to dance, and Weevil grabbed it. 'That's Gnat's signal that he's reached the ledge,' she explained. 'We need to go up before the sun comes down.'

'Get moving,' said Ludicra.

Weevil grabbed the rope and nimbly scaled the wall, vanishing into the reddish mist above them. Ludicra only hoped she would climb half as well as the lanky ogre.

When the rope danced again, Ludicra grabbed it and gave it a good pull. If it was going to break, it would break on her. Grunting, she hauled her bulk upward. Before starting on this mad quest, Ludicra had been the most spoiled troll in the Dismal Swamp, and she couldn't have done this climb. Now she willed herself to go higher, even as she had willed her makeshift band to rescue Rollo.

Grunting, groaning, and sweating all over, Ludicra finally got to a point where Weevil could haul her onto a narrow ledge. Her heart leaped, because this much of Dwayne's treasure map was true! She, Weevil, and Gnat pressed against the cliff face and stared over the edge – it was a long way down into swirling red mists and fiery sludge. All three of them gazed up and around, trying to find the elusive Troll Treasure.

All Ludicra could see of interest was a tree limb, or root, which grew from the side of the cliff farther up. At the tip of this limb was a large blob, like a hornet's nest. But it was so high up, it was difficult to judge the size of this strange nest.

'Is that full of bees?' Weevil asked nervously. 'I hate bees. Their stingers get stuck in your teeth.'

'I know,' answered Ludicra, who didn't like to eat

live bees either. 'But if you get them when it's cold and rainy, they're sluggish and—'

'Will you two shut up!' snapped Gnat. 'The sun is coming down the canyon.'

Sure enough, daylight flowed into the dark, misty gorge like a flood of water, bathing everything in cheerful bright colors. The plants opened their leaves and blossoms until they no longer looked like scrawny weeds. Then sunlight raced up their side of the chasm, and it struck the hornet's nest with blazing intensity. Ludicra, Gnat, and Weevil all gasped in awe.

When the sun struck the massive nest, it turned into a dazzling ball of golden vessels, gleaming diamonds, bejeweled crowns, doubloons, and pearl necklaces. The treasure clump was far away, but the gold shimmered as if it were in Ludicra's grasp. The baubles glistened like fireflies in the middle of the day.

Gazing at this wonder, Ludicra guessed that the nest had been built and rebuilt from saliva and found objects over many centuries. Now it was the greatest hoard in the world, all stuck together like the stuff in an ogre's hairball. She could now see the ancient tree that supported the limb and the nest. It grew from a second ledge about fifty feet above them.

The loot wasn't alone. They watched in amazement as colorful winged reptiles flitted to and from the nest. The sleek creatures were about troll size, and Ludicra realized she had met three of them last night at the watering hole.

Gnat gulped. 'Are those what I think they are?'

'Dragons,' breathed Ludicra. 'I met them last night.'

'Aren't they a bit small for dragons?' asked Crawfleece.

'There may be bigger ones about,' answered Ludicra, looking around nervously.

Weevil sighed. 'So that's why the elves can't get the treasure. How are *we* going to get it? Cut it loose, and it will fall into the lava.'

'If we could even get up there,' added Gnat, 'without a flying troll.'

'We're fresh out of flying trolls,' muttered Weevil.

After a few more seconds of gaping Gnat said, 'That is tremendous. It's almost too fantastic to steal, if you know what I mean.'

Ludicra and Weevil nodded, because they knew what the gnome meant. The treasure trove was home to these little dragons, and it was somehow too wonderful to disturb.

'Stygius Rex won't have any trouble stealing it,' said Weevil. 'He won't feel sorry for the little dragons. And he can fly.'

'So do we go back and tell him about it?' asked Ludicra, feeling defeated.

A large bird swooped overhead. *It's probably spying on the elves*, thought Ludicra. At once the ravenous dragons darted toward the bird and fell upon it, tearing it apart in seconds. A tiny shower of feathers drifted down and sizzled as they hit the lava.

The flying creatures also caught lizards on the rock face and ate them. They drank from a spring near the gnarled tree and inspected the visitors from a distance. All too quickly the show was over when the sunlight stole away, rising up the side of the canyon until they were left in red-hued darkness. Once again the treasure was a gray blob hanging on a tree limb.

'That was beautiful!' exclaimed Gnat. 'But it might as well be on the moon.'

Weevil bowed apologetically to Ludicra. 'Your elf spoke the truth.'

'A lie would almost have been kinder,' muttered the troll. 'How are we going to get that loot? Even if we do get it, how are we going to bring it home? I asked before . . . should we tell Stygius Rex and be done with it?'

'I don't know,' answered Weevil, 'but we'd better hurry up. Look down there.' The ogre pointed toward the bottom of the chasm, where elves were sneaking through the bushes, surrounding Captain Chomp and Crawfleece. Their comrades couldn't even see the threat.

'Weevil, can you shoot an arrow that far?' asked Ludicra.

The ogre nodded as she strung her bow. 'I can, but I don't know how accurate I'll be.'

'Just protect our friends, if you can,' said Ludicra. The troll knelt down and grabbed the rope.

'Where are you going?' asked Gnat.

'To talk to Dwayne and the elves.' Ludicra swung herself off the ledge and carefully began to shimmy down the rope. Halfway to the bottom a breeze began to fan the troll's hide, and she turned her head to see Clipper fluttering beside her.

Oh no! thought Ludicra. *That stupid fairy's going to tickle me or make me sneeze!*

'Go away!' begged the troll. 'Don't torment me!'

'No, I would never hurt you,' said the fairy with pain in her lilting voice. 'I mean, I suppose I might have hurt you before, but ... I don't feel like that anymore.'

'What do you mean, you don't feel like that?' asked the troll as she tried to get to the ground as quickly as possible.

'Something has changed in me,' said the fairy with wonder and gratitude in her voice. 'After the knife was destroyed in the lava, I couldn't remember for the longest time who I was. I just flew and flew – straight up the chasm. You know, I was almost at the top before I remembered who I was.' The fairy's eyes lit up with shock. 'I had *died*!'

'But you didn't have the decency to stay dead,' Ludicra commented.

Clipper nodded her head. 'I know! It was that cursed knife that brought me back, but it's been destroyed – really!'

'Really?' Ludicra lowered herself claw over claw, trying to get to the ground. As long as she kept the fairy talking, she had a chance to make it down alive. 'You won't mind if I think this is some kind of nasty trick ... like you always play?'

'Ludicra, I'm not evil anymore!' insisted the delicate flyer. 'The knife made me bad, but destroying it made me *good* again. Does that make sense?'

'I guess so.' Ludicra didn't sound convinced.

'Where is Rollo?' asked Clipper urgently.

That question brought a stab of pain to the troll's

heart. 'I don't know. He flew off to—' She decided not to finish the sentence.

'We need him!'

'I can't argue that,' said Ludicra. With relief she dropped to the ground. She pulled her club from her backpack, ready to bash the fey being . . . but Clipper was gone. Ludicra rubbed her eyes, wondering if that conversation had really happened. Was it possible Clipper was no longer a demonic henchfairy?

'Pssst!' hissed a voice. 'Over here!'

The troll turned to see Captain Chomp waving to her from behind a boulder on the far side of the pool. With a quick look around Ludicra hurried to his position. 'You've got elves surrounding you,' she whispered.

'I can smell them,' muttered the ogre. 'Did you see it? The treasure?'

She nodded somberly. 'It's real. But the elves are right – it would take a miracle to get it. It's all entwined in a dragon's nest, on a tree growing high up the cliff.'

'Ewww!' said another voice in the darkness. It was Crawfleece. 'So what are we going to do?'

'I'm going to talk to Dwayne.' The troll shook her head. 'Maybe if we worked together—'

Without warning a net dropped over her head, ensnaring Ludicra along with Captain Chomp. There came brusque orders, and elves surrounded them, bows ready. Chomp blustered and shouted, but there wasn't much either of them could do. Ludicra looked around for Crawfleece, but she didn't see the big troll.

I hope she escaped, thought Ludicra.

It was difficult to stand up, especially with Chomp

struggling, and she didn't want to give the elves reason to shoot. 'Sit down,' Ludicra ordered the ogre as she plopped to the ground. 'Just relax. We need to talk to them, anyway.'

The ogre had some choice words for their captors; then he dropped his club and settled to the ground.

'That's better,' said Dwayne. The elf stepped forward into the reddish light, and he was without his usual charming smile. 'You promise not to fight us?'

'I was coming to see you,' answered Ludicra. 'You didn't have to do this. I got a good look at it in the sun.'

Dwayne scowled. 'Why did you set those traps for us?'

She shrugged. 'Why did you set traps for us in the tunnel? Why did you send spies to follow us? You don't trust us; we don't trust you. But it doesn't matter, because neither one of us can get that treasure.'

'Stand down.' Dwayne motioned to his band of elves to lower their bows, and reluctantly they did. 'You can get it – you have flying ogres and trolls and wizards. All we have are puny fairies.'

'We're out of flying trolls and ogres,' answered Ludicra sadly. 'And Stygius Rex is not really on our side.'

'Let us out of here, you pipsqueak!' roared Captain Chomp, shaking his fist. 'Poison arrows, nets, traps – elves are gutless wonders who won't fight claw-to-claw!'

'Ssshh!' cautioned Ludicra. 'That won't make things any better.'

Dwayne frowned and said, 'I told you the truth about

the treasure. You wanted to know, and now you know. The treasure's on *our* side of the chasm, so you and your foul folk can just leave!'

That bristled the hair on Ludicra's neck. 'I don't think you know where all of my band is. Until Stygius Rex is defeated, we'll be after that treasure.'

She hoped Weevil and Gnat had pulled up the rope when they saw that she and Chomp had been captured.

'You dislike the mage that much?' asked Dwayne, rubbing his chin. 'If he were eliminated, you would leave us alone?'

'In a squish,' answered Ludicra. 'That's the only reason we're still here in this smelly gorge. Stygius Rex won't let us leave – unless we give him the treasure.'

Chomp growled. 'Even then he'll try to cheat us.'

'What good is a bunch of golden goblets and diamond tiaras?' asked Ludicra. 'We're trolls and ogres, not elves. Some grubs or a nice deposit of mushrooms – *that* would be a treasure.'

'Speak for yourself,' said Chomp. 'I'd look good in a diamond tiara.'

At that remark Dwayne was forced to smile. 'Cut them loose,' he told his minions.

The elves didn't move right away, and some of them lifted their bows in caution. Dwayne glared at his underlings, and they finally began to free the prisoners from the nets.

Ludicra had no sooner staggered to her feet than a howl of fury came from the fog. Two enraged ogres stormed into the gathering and began to bash the surprised elves right and left. They clobbered one after another, but the elves had the numbers and fought back. Ludicra ducked out of the way, although Captain Chomp grabbed his club and joined in the melee.

Ludicra didn't recognize these two ogres. Both of them were very burned, and one of them wore a smudged metal bowl on his head. The elves dared not shoot their arrows wildly, for fear of hitting one another. So the outnumbered ogres were winning the battle.

Ludicra muttered angrily. These bumbling strangers had arrived just in time to start the war between Bonespittle and the Bonny Woods all over again!

THIRTEEN

Dragon's Nest

Filbum and Stygius Rex perched atop a large black boulder, watching the battle between the ogres and the elves from a safe distance. The ogres were outnumbered, but the elves had been taken by surprise as they were letting some other ogres go. At least, that's what Filbum thought he saw in the red shadows and churning fog. The grunts and groans and thuds were clear enough.

'Shouldn't we go rescue them?' asked Filbum in alarm.

Stygius Rex shuddered at the idea. 'I don't know – they look so *violent* to me. Besides, which ones do you think need rescuing?'

Filbum shrugged. 'They both do!'

The old mage lifted his head and peered into the steamy darkness. 'You know, my eyes are still pretty good. I think I see some more of your band on that ledge above the pool. What is that above them . . . a tree?'

Filbum shook his shaggy head because he couldn't see anything but big shapes fighting little shapes. They had arrived just after the sunlight had fled the canyon, and they were being cautious. Still, Filbum felt as if he ought to be doing *something* to help the situation. He had freed the hostages, but he wasn't sure whether Stygius Rex's transformation was real or not.

Suddenly a shimmering image floated in front of the troll, and he almost fell off the rock. The sorcerer had to catch him, and Stygius Rex was beaming when he set Filbum upright. 'It's my old friend Clipper!' he exclaimed. 'How are you, my dear?'

The fairy stared suspiciously at the cadaverous mage. Then she shrugged and said, 'You're noble now. Do you know why?'

'Pray tell, why?' asked the wizard, leaning forward with interest.

'Because the black serpent knife was destroyed.'

Stygius Rex nodded sagely. 'Ah! I wondered about that. Those turned evil by the cursed knife are turned good when it's destroyed. I was evil before dying and coming back, but somehow it still worked.'

'So will you stop that fighting down there?' asked Filbum, pointing to the melee in the canyon.

'Do you think a fireball would do it?' asked the wizard with concern. 'I don't want to accidentally harm anyone.'

Clipper darted back in front of Filbum. 'Where is Rollo?' she demanded. 'No one else seems to know!'

'*I* know,' answered Filbum glumly. 'A huge dragon carried us to the end of the Great Chasm, where the lava meets a swamp. There's a meadow and a stone hut, and I left him in a secret room in the hut. If he went through the portal as I did, he's in Bonespittle.'

The fairy looked stricken. 'You are the trolls who met Batmole?'

'Batmole?' asked Stygius Rex in alarm. He cringed and began to tremble. 'Is that dreadful mage still alive? If so, we should get out of here!'

The sorcerer started to fly away, but Filbum grabbed him and hauled him back to the boulder. 'Not so fast, Rex. You started this mess, and you have to finish it. What if we gave this Batmole character the treasure?'

'Oh, he'll take the treasure,' answered Clipper. 'What he really wanted was the black knife and revenge on Stygius Rex – for killing all the other sorcerers.'

'I was terribly naughty, wasn't I?' wailed the mage, who seemed all of his thousand-plus years. 'Can't Batmole see that I've changed? I only want to help Rollo now.'

'I don't think he cares about Rollo,' said Clipper. 'He's upset that he didn't get the knife.'

The old wizard looked remorseful, and Filbum shook him by his scrawny shoulders. 'Come on, Rex, snap out of it! There're a lot of things we have to do to make it turn out right.'

'Batmole is back,' said Stygius Rex, shaking his head fearfully. 'He was the greatest of us all. Nobody else could have created all of *this*.' He motioned around at the dismal gorge filled with lava, fetid gases, and gnome-eating plants. Grunts, groans, and thunks sounded from the battle below.

'Yeah, great achievement,' answered Clipper. 'Somebody has to stop that fighting down there.

There're six elves on one ogre, and they're still getting pummeled. Mage, we could use a fireball.'

Stygius Rex sniffed back his tears. 'I feel just *awful* about all the things I've done, and now you want me to throw a fireball?'

'Yes, and quickly,' suggested Filbum.

Looking stricken with guilt, the sobbing sorcerer conjured up a fireball that blazed like a miniature sun. With a flick of his wrist it streaked down the canyon into the middle of the combatants, where it exploded with ferocious force. Elves and ogres alike were thrown into the air, their pelts aflame. Almost all of them had to jump into the pool to escape the firestorm as a cloud of gray smoke drifted upward from the smoldering thickets.

'Nice one,' said Filbum with admiration. 'You're getting better at this now that you're on the right side.'

'Still, I am no match for Batmole,' muttered the mage. 'Let's make peace and get out of here before he arrives.'

Ludicra was dazed, but she could feel someone dragging her through the smoking rubble. Everyone was bent over coughing, or running around in flames until they could jump into the pool. Not only was the lava burning, but so was everything else.

'That old buzzard uncorked a good one that time,' muttered a familiar voice between labored grunts.

Ludicra looked up to see Crawfleece huffing away as she dragged her to safety. 'Your pelt's on fire,' added Rollo's sister.

'Thanks,' wheezed Ludicra. She patted her smoldering fur and tried to focus her thoughts. The impact of the massive fireball had knocked her out, but only for a second. She could remember the melee in the fog – lovely elves fighting singed ogres – but she had been trying to make peace. Then the fireball hit.

'Let me up!' Ludicra knocked away Crawfleece's paws and lumbered to her feet. 'If Stygius Rex is here, he knows where the treasure is! We've got to get back to the ledge.'

The two trolls scrambled through the burning embers, smoke, and wailing elves until they reached the cliff Ludicra had climbed earlier. The rope was gone, but she could see the first piton just above her head. The ledge was hidden in smoke and mist. 'Weevil!' she shouted over the din. 'It's Ludicra! Let me up!'

'Let *us* up!' bellowed Crawfleece. 'Hurry.'

The elves were beginning to collect themselves, but Captain Chomp had disappeared, as had the two strange ogres. The rope flopped down to the ground just as an elf retrieved his bow and began to look for an arrow.

'Go!' Ludicra told Crawfleece, pushing her toward the rope.

The big troll nodded and started to climb, urged on by her comrades above them. Ludicra kept her eye on the elf, and when she saw him pick up an arrow, she was about to charge him. Upon seeing that the shaft was broken, he scowled, and she shook her fist at him. When the rope danced again, the troll eagerly grabbed it and began to climb.

Fortunately it was dark, and smoke and swirling embers floated all around them, mixed with the usual steam and noxious gases. So Ludicra wasn't far off the ground before she became invisible from below. Her companions pulled her over the ledge and helped her up, and the leader took stock of their situation.

They were on a narrow ledge about halfway to the old tree and treasure-laden nest. It grew from a second ledge, which they could reach if they had enough pitons and more guts than brains. Ludicra couldn't see the dragons in the dark, but she knew they were somewhere close to the nest.

She looked at her comrades on the dangerous ledge. Crawfleece, Weevil, and Gnat – they were all that was left of her once mighty band. Rollo, Filbum, and so many ogres, including Captain Chomp, had gone missing.

Reading her mind, Weevil asked, 'Where is Captain Chomp?'

Ludicra heaved her beefy shoulder. 'When I last saw him, he was fighting alongside two ogres who charged out of nowhere to attack the elves. One of them had a metal bowl on his head.'

'Sergeant Skull,' breathed Weevil with distaste. 'If Stygius Rex is here, that makes sense. But why did he throw a fireball at his own ogres?'

'All I know is that the treasure is above us,' answered the troll, pointing to the blob in the mist. 'Who wants to get it?'

'I do!' said Gnat excitedly.

With a frown Weevil nodded. 'I guess I will.'

Crawfleece gazed upward and shook her head. 'What treasure?'

'That nest up there is full of golden baubles and jewels,' Gnat answered gleefully. 'You can only see them when the sun hits, but they're in that clump. *We've* seen it.'

'It's real,' agreed Weevil, 'and so is the danger.'

'But we've got all night, and it's a long night!' insisted Gnat. 'Who else is going to get there ahead of us?'

Suddenly a dark, slender figure cut through the mist over their heads and veered upward toward the dragon's nest. From the flapping cloak Ludicra knew it was Stygius Rex. He had already announced his presence with the fireball, and his powers seemed to be getting stronger.

'It's *him*!' hissed Crawfleece.

Weevil quickly strung her bow.

'No, wait,' whispered Ludicra. 'He probably doesn't know we're here. He hasn't seen the dragons yet, or they haven't seen him. He's just looking – he can't get the treasure down or carry it away.'

Weevil lowered her bow and scowled. 'What if he makes it float up to the rim?'

'Can he do that?' squeaked Gnat.

They all turned their attention to the dark figure hovering in front of the mysterious tree. He raised his arms as he floated, and the golden baubles began to tinkle, like the most delicate wind chimes. It did seem as if he could make the entire clump move, and Weevil lifted her bow. At this distance, with the mist, thought Ludicra, she would be lucky to hit him.

'Um,' said Gnat, 'we don't really need a fireball right on top of us. There's no place to run on this ledge.'

'Hold your fire,' said Crawfleece. 'I saw—'

Out of nowhere flying shapes swirled around the mage, and he waved his arms like a banshee to get rid of them. As the small dragons pecked and ripped at him, Stygius Rex dove back to the boulders and tried to find cover. He finally crashed to the ground, where they tormented him until he staggered to his feet. The sorcerer threw up his arms, which caused the dragons to fly backward as if put into reverse.

Ludicra was distracted by more activity on the ground – in the bushes and shadows, almost everywhere. There was no fighting, but there were plenty of elves skulking around, dragging off their injured. The troll looked for the mage and the small dragons, but they were gone from her sight. At least his first effort to get the treasure had been repelled.

Gnat breathed a loud sigh of relief. 'Okay, we had better make our move,' said the gnome. 'I've counted up our pitons, and we don't have enough . . . unless we pull up the ones below.'

'Then how do we get down?' asked Crawfleece.

'I don't know,' answered the gnome, 'but we'll have the treasure!'

'Can't we just saw off the limb?' asked Weevil.

'And let it all crash to the ground?' Ludicra shook her head doubtfully. 'I think we'd lose half of it in the lava.'

'If you all worked together you could get it,' squeaked a little voice somewhere out in the mist. They all jumped with fright, and Crawfleece swung her club at a shadow and almost fell off the ledge. Weevil and Ludicra caught her and pulled her back.

The voice laughed. 'Trolls are still funny. Good!'

'Why is that good?' demanded Crawfleece. 'Is that Clipper?'

'Yes, but I'm not going to show myself until you

calm down. I'm not the enemy anymore. I've turned *good*, and so has Stygius Rex.'

'Right, and I'm the mayor of Fungus Meadow,' said Ludicra snidely. 'We just saw him get dragon-pecked . . . while trying to get the treasure.'

'He thought if he could present it to everyone, it would bring peace,' answered the fairy, revealing herself in the mist. 'His plans haven't worked out lately.'

'If you really want to be friendly,' said Ludicra, 'just go away. We're not interested in working with you.'

'The black knife was destroyed,' said the fairy, flitting closer. 'Really, we're both noble now. If you won't believe *me*, will you believe Filbum?'

'Filbum?' echoed Crawfleece, clutching her hairy chest. 'Is my darling all right?'

'Yes, he was quite heroic when he rescued Nulneck and Krunkle,' answered the fairy. 'It's a long story . . . If you come down, we can tell you.'

'It's a trick,' cautioned Weevil.

'Where has he been?' asked Crawfleece suspiciously.

'To the end of the chasm, to Bonespittle, down the tunnel — a million different places!' The fairy waved her arms to encompass the whole world. 'Just now, he's hiding in the rocks, nursing Stygius Rex.'

'This is just slowing us up!' complained Gnat. He waved at the fairy and barked, 'Get out of here!'

Ludicra remembered something important. 'You ran off to get the black knife for someone . . . who? Gnat and I saw you talking to him.'

'That would be Batmole,' answered Clipper. 'In fact, it would be wise to go before he —'

'Too late,' said Weevil, pointing down into the fiery gorge. 'Something big is happening.'

Holding her breath, Ludicra gazed over the ledge and saw a long line of elves emerging from the bushes. They were using the trail that her band had carved through the thickets. As she peered closer, she could see the elves were all carrying rods over their heads, and these rods were attached to one another.

'It's a ladder!' said Weevil with amazement. 'Like a siege ladder, only much longer. That's what they were hammering and trying to hide from us when we snuck past them. A big ladder!'

Gnat snorted. '*That* won't reach the treasure.'

'Maybe not,' said Ludicra, 'but it will reach this ledge. Then they run it from this ledge to the next one . . . and get the treasure.'

'They're not as dumb as they look,' said Weevil.

'I want to know about my Filbum!' screeched Crawfleece. The troll looked for the fairy but couldn't find her. 'Clipper! Clipper! Where are you?'

'Just hope she was telling the truth,' said Ludicra.

A few elves carefully leaned the immense ladder against the cliff, while others leveled their bows and stood guard. Ludicra looked for Dwayne, hoping he hadn't been hurt in the fighting, but she couldn't tell one elf from another in the dark.

When the elves had actually placed the ladder against the cliff, they were not lined up to reach the first ledge. They would be high enough, but about twenty feet away.

'Don't they know where the ledge is?' asked Gnat. 'Stupid elves.'

'They must know we're up here,' answered Weevil. 'So they're not going to send the ladder right up to us. We'd kick it away.'

Elves, one after another, began to climb the ladder, until about six of them were headed up. The rest stood guard below. The trolls, ogre, and gnome peered at the approaching foes and wondered what they were doing.

Ludicra realized they all had bows on their backs. 'They'll shoot us with poison arrows,' she insisted. 'We need a plan!'

'What can we do?' asked Crawfleece through her tears. 'We're sitting up on this ledge like targets at a worm-spitting contest.'

'I've got a few arrows left,' said Weevil, grabbing her bow. 'I'll make the most of them.'

'Dwayne never mentioned his stupid ladder,' grumbled Ludicra, sounding hurt. 'Why did he need *us*?'

'To make that trail,' answered Gnat.

The elves climbed relentlessly higher until they were about twenty feet away. Clinging to the ladder, they were stacked like the heads on a totem pole. They swayed in the wind, but the lightweight elves were still able to string their bows and prepare to shoot.

Weevil had a jump on them, and she got off the first arrow, which whistled past the ear of the top archer. He shot one in return, which clattered off the rock behind them. Soon all six elven archers were firing at will, and the Bonespittlians huddled on the narrow ledge, unable to protect themselves.

One scratch from those arrows, thought Ludicra, *and we're dead.*

FOURTEEN

Showdown

The elf on top of the ladder suddenly sneezed. A moment later all six of the elves who had been shooting at Ludicra and her band started sneezing out of control. This didn't cause them to fall off the incredibly high ladder, but it gave those on the ledge a chance to react.

Weevil jumped up and shot an arrow, which got the top elf in the shoulder. He dropped his bow and gripped the ladder, even while he kept sneezing.

'Gnat, give me a length of rope,' ordered Ludicra. 'Have you got a grappling hook?'

'Right here,' answered the gnome, instantly realizing what the troll wanted to do. He tied their best hook onto his best length of rope and handed it to her.

'Stand back,' ordered Ludicra, pushing her companions out of the way. She dropped the rope over the ledge and began to swing the hook back and forth, hoping to get it high enough to catch the ladder. With every whoosh, the hook got closer to its target.

One of the sneezing elves tried to shoot an arrow, but it fell short. Weevil got off a shot and hit an elf in the leg. Their attack was falling apart, and the lowest elf tried to climb down to stop Ludicra from hooking the ladder.

She hit the wooden rail twice before the hook finally caught a rung. 'Pull!' she said, handing the rope to her companions.

They pulled, dragging the ladder across the cliff face, forcing the elves lower with every inch. Now the fey folk dropped their bows and slid down as fast as they could. Most of them got to the ground before the ladder toppled over and broke. A broken section of ladder hung from their hook like a dead sucker fish.

'Hurrah!' shouted Weevil.

Crawfleece laughed. 'Look at them run!'

'Nice shooting, Weevil!' exclaimed Gnat. 'That showed those stupid elves!'

But Ludicra was not cheering or yelling – she was frowning with concern. 'We can't go on like this,' she muttered. 'I've got to go talk to Dwayne.'

'They'll use you for a pincushion,' warned Crawfleece. 'They just tried to kill us.'

'I know,' said Ludicra, 'but they think we attacked them with those two strange trolls.'

'After they threw nets over us,' replied Crawfleece.

'Okay, things aren't going well.' Ludicra grabbed

the climbing rope and was about to throw it down, when Clipper darted in front of her.

'I can still make 'em sneeze!' bragged the fairy. 'Ludicra, please wait. Don't go anywhere.'

The fairy turned to Crawfleece. 'Filbum says that you talked about having your wedding at the Hole in the Forbidden Forest. So you can swing on the vines, like you love to do. *Now* do you believe that I'm on your side?'

With a shriek Crawfleece clapped her hands. 'My Filbum is all right! Thank you for telling me, Clipper. Where is he? When can I see him?'

The fairy glanced toward the bottom, where the elven band was regrouping. 'I don't suggest you go down now – the elves are steaming mad. Stygius Rex must do something to end the fight because he's the only one who can get them all to stop and listen. We can split the treasure – we can live in peace.'

'Where are the other ogres?' asked Ludicra.

Clipper frowned. 'The elves have taken them prisoner. Two of them are burned.'

'So we just sit here, waiting?' asked Crawfleece impatiently. 'I want to see Filbum!'

'I want the treasure,' said Gnat. The gnome leaned over the ledge and looked at the chunk of ladder hanging from their hook. 'Hey, I've got an idea! Weevil, can you stick that grappling hook onto an arrow and shoot it up to the tree, with the rope attached? If you can, we could climb up there. We could even make a pulley to lower the treasure down.'

'I could try,' answered Weevil. She grabbed the rope

and started to haul the hook and ladder back to the ledge.

Ludicra peered upward into the reddish shadows – she couldn't see anything moving. 'It appears as if the dragons have flown off. Hurry . . . before somebody else tries something crazy.'

'I wish Rollo were here,' said Clipper wistfully.

'Me too,' agreed Ludicra. 'Me too.'

From the top of the boulder, Filbum watched the elves scurrying around, trying to regroup after their failed attempt with the ladder. He couldn't tell what had happened up there on the side of the cliff, but he hoped his friends were safe, especially Crawfleece.

Ever since Clipper had reported that the band was alive and near the treasure, he had been worrying. Too many weird things were going on, and too many people wanted that trove.

Filbum glanced back at the crestfallen sorcerer, sitting a few feet away. Ever since his own failure, Stygius Rex had just stared into space and nursed his wounds. He was noble now, but he had lost a certain edge to his confidence. It bothered him terribly to hurt any creature, even dragons, elves, and Sergeant Skull. If he stepped on a worm, he would probably be this remorseful.

'Rex, you've got to do something,' said Filbum. 'Until yesterday this place was the best-kept secret in two lands. Now it's busier here than Dismal Swamp on a holiday.'

'It's all my fault,' muttered the distraught mage. 'If

only I hadn't been so greedy. If only I hadn't killed everybody or turned them into slaves.'

'Nobody's perfect,' said Filbum. 'The question is, what will you do to end this stand-off? Whatever it is, you're going to have to act like the *old* Stygius Rex, or no one will listen to you. Warm and fuzzy won't work with these hard heads.'

The mage blinked tearfully at him. 'If I tell the elves they can have the stupid treasure, if I tell the trolls and ogres to go home, all is forgiven . . . will they obey me?'

'It's worth a try,' answered Filbum.

The sorcerer nodded as if making up his mind; then he rose to his full stooped height and conjured another fireball. This one he let dance in his outstretched palm until he hurled it high into the air. The missile exploded in a shower of sparks that lit up the yellow clouds like the rising sun. That got everyone's attention.

The elves dove for cover, but Filbum could see their pointed ears poking up from the bushes. 'Listen, everyone!' declared Stygius Rex in a voice that almost sounded like the old scoundrel. 'We have to stop this fighting. If the elves will let those from Bonespittle leave peacefully, they can *have* the troll treasure.'

He cleared his throat. 'Any ogre, troll, or gnome who returns home will be forgiven . . . whatever he's done. We're going to start fresh, with a new king. Not *me*!'

'Don't let them think you're weak,' whispered Filbum. 'Tell them, "Do what I say, or you'll be punished."'

'Do what he says, or I'll be punished!' announced Stygius Rex, pointing to Filbum. Then he shook his head with confusion and added, 'Elves, just back off to a safe distance and let us leave. You can have it all!'

'How can we believe you?' shouted a fair-haired elf who had to be Dwayne. 'You've tried to trick us and trap us every step of the way. You sent flying ogres and trolls after us – you started a war in the Bonny Woods. You have been the worst thing that ever happened to us!'

The old sorcerer looked apologetic, and he said, 'I only wanted to unite our two lands. Let the treasure be repayment for the wrongs we have done you!'

'Not so fast!' cried another voice, and everyone turned to look at a boulder on the other side of the lava river. There stood a smaller black-robed figure. He crossed his arms and scowled angrily. 'That treasure happens to belong to *me*! It was on its way to me when it was stolen.'

'Batmole?' Stygius Rex asked nervously. He forced a pained smile. 'Long time no see! How have you been?'

'Better than my fellow sorcerers, you vile murderer!' yelled Batmole. 'It wasn't enough to kill them. You had to use the black knife to bring them back as *ghouls*! To be your slaves.'

Stygius Rex cringed. 'The ghouls didn't remember their previous lives, and I made slaves of *everyone* in Bonespittle.' He sighed, and his shoulders slumped. 'All right, I'm vile ... or I used to be vile. Now I'm trying to make amends and do a noble act. Don't you see that making the Great Chasm was also vile? That has kept us from knowing each other. Let's give the treasure to the elves as a peace offering!'

'It's *mine*!' roared the shorter mage, stepping forward. 'But first I have to take care of *you*.'

The squat sorcerer rolled up his sleeves, and a clap of thunder sounded high overhead. That was followed by a lightning bolt that streaked down the center of the chasm and headed straight for Stygius Rex. If Filbum hadn't scrambled to his feet and tackled Stygius Rex, the old mage would have been killed on the spot. The lightning bolt struck the boulder with a tremendous explosion and split it in two, as Filbum and Stygius Rex were hurled to the ground.

Now the elves were voluntarily getting out of the way, running in every direction. Wiping sand from his face and clothes, Stygius Rex staggered to his feet. 'I'm nice now,' he sputtered, 'but I'm not *that* nice!'

He waved his hand, and a massive fireball materialized and shot across the river of lava. Batmole leaped off the boulder just as the flaming missile struck and exploded in a shower of sparks and embers.

The little mage jumped to his feet and began to shriek, 'I'll fix you! Take this!' The ground began to rumble, and every geyser in the Great Chasm shot off at once. The lava split off from the river and began to run through the plants, turning them into an inferno. Rocks fell from the cliffs high above, and even the ogres were screaming. It was a full-scale earthquake!

Stygius Rex turned to Filbum and gasped. 'Now what do I do?'

'Attack him!' begged the troll. Stygius Rex nodded and shuffled into the mist.

Filbum jumped on a rock and looked around the

chaotic canyon, trying to find Crawfleece. Smoke, dust, and steam filled the air, and it was impossible to see anything. Even so, Stygius Rex flung another fireball, which blasted across the lava and exploded where Batmole had been standing a moment ago. To the troll's great relief, the earthquake stopped.

'Crawfleece!' yelled Filbum. 'Crawfleece, where are you?'

At that moment Crawfleece was trying to hold on to a rope that had a heavy troll swinging from the other end. Weevil and Gnat rushed to help her, but the three of them couldn't control Ludicra as she whooshed back and forth like a great pendulum.

Weevil had shot the grappling hook onto the high tree limb, where it stuck. Ludicra had insisted upon climbing, and she had almost reached the dragon's nest when the fireworks started below them. With the rumbling of the earthquake Ludicra had lost her grip and was swinging back and forth on their safety line, which was wrapped around the tree limb and tied to her ample waist.

Ludicra swung to and fro, watching the smoke and flames swirling beneath her. Then came another lightning bolt, ripping through the chasm to explode in a searing blast of heat. That was followed by a golden fireball that arced into the lava and blew molten magma a hundred feet into the air. Blobs of fire rained upon everyone, and it seemed as if the whole world were ending!

Even the dragons were afraid. Ludicra could see them

circling warily overhead, or maybe they were just waiting to attack her.

'Let me down!' cried Ludicra.

'We can't!' answered Crawfleece. 'We're barely holding on. You're going to drag us off the ledge!'

Something moved in front of the helpless troll, and she saw a dark cloak rippling in the smoky wind. She gasped when she saw it was Batmole. He paid little attention to her as he hovered in front of the cluster of jewels and gold. Laughing, he counted the loot and rubbed his hands together. He spoke some strange words, and the clump of treasure began to rattle, like pots and pans hanging on a line.

Out of the swirling fog zoomed another dark figure, which crashed into Batmole and slammed him against the cliff. It was Stygius Rex, and the two sorcerers grappled in midair like two hawks fighting over the same sparrow. Lightning flashed, thunder roared, earthquakes shook the chasm, and a fireball spun like a corkscrew into the sky. Rain and hail battered the combatants, and Ludicra didn't think anyone would survive the vicious battle.

A bolt of lightning struck Stygius Rex in the back, and he plummeted from the sky, his cloak on fire. He dropped through the mist and landed in the burning rubble below them.

'The treasure is mine!' crowed Batmole in triumph. He looked directly at Ludicra and sneered. 'Trolls, you are done causing me trouble. I don't like *any* of you. I'm going to do what I should have done a thousand years ago – wipe out Bonespittle!'

Ludicra began flailing her arms, trying to reach her comrades, but all she could do was swing close to the ledge where they stood. 'Pull me up to the tree!' she shouted.

Weevil, Crawfleece, and Gnat tugged with all their might on the rope, and Ludicra rose slowly back to the tree. Batmole glanced at her, then went back to inspecting his treasure. He waved, and a brilliant sapphire necklace separated itself from the clump and floated out to his hand.

With her friends pulling on the rope, Ludicra rose until her head bonked against the thick tree branch. Shaking off the pain, she twisted around and tried to grab the trunk. After three tries she finally got a hand-hold, and her companions could release their tension on the rope.

Of course, the troll was hardly safe. She was hanging from a tree a hundred feet up the side of a cliff – with a deranged sorcerer glaring at her. Rain and hail pelted her, and the Great Chasm shook like leech jelly from all the quakes.

'How should I do this?' asked Batmole cheerfully. 'I'll just make the tree fall out.' He waved his hands again, and the dirt began to crumble away from the tree roots. When Ludicra felt the branches shifting under her weight, she scrambled back to the ledge where the tree was rooted.

Squawking sounded high overhead, and Ludicra looked up to see the small dragons circling frantically. *Are they worried about their nest?* she wondered. *They should be!* In another second, it would all come tumbling down.

Batmole sneezed and dropped the necklace he'd been holding, and the ground stopped shaking. The mage began to scratch his back, itching frantically; he whirled around, looking for Clipper. The winsome fairy darted down and grabbed the necklace as it fell into the chasm. She lifted the jewelry and used it to deflect a weak lightning bolt as Batmole sneezed again.

'Curse you, nasty little sprite!' he sniffed. 'I'll level the Bonny Woods too!'

Clipper caught Ludicra's eye and pointed upward; then the fey being dashed out of sight. The troll looked up to see the small dragons flying merrily and squeaking happily, which seemed odd. Then a great black shape blotted out all the flaming sparks and lava-lit fog, and it descended upon them like an eclipse of the moon.

Ludicra blinked in amazement, because the apparition wasn't alone. Bathed in fog, a two-legged creature hung from the monster's talons, and then crashed into the tree just above her and slid down.

'Whoa! Hey!' cried a familiar voice.

'Rollo!' she shrieked as the troll flew by her and landed on top of the treasure nest.

Everyone in the smoky canyon – troll, ogre, and elf – rose to their feet and watched the mother dragon make a lazy circle through the mist. Flapping her wings slowly, she turned and dove straight toward Batmole, who was still hovering in front of her nest. There was a flash of recognition in her turquoise eyes, plus anger, as if bad blood had passed between them before.

The sorcerer looked frantically for an escape route,

but there was nothing around him except air and rock. 'I didn't mean it! Please don't—'

Batmole leveled a lightning bolt at the dragon just as he sneezed, and the missile veered off course. The flying serpent bore down on her target, who made a desperate dash up the cliff face. With a flick of her wings the behemoth changed course and speared Batmole in the chest with a monstrous talon. In her other claw she gripped a golden cup, which Ludicra imagined she was bringing home to the nest.

With her prizes clutched in her talons, the beast made a triumphant cry. Then she flapped her mighty wings and zoomed upward, with the smoke swirling behind her. Chirping happily, the baby dragons all followed, and soon there was silence in the blasted, smoldering chasm.

There was silence, except for the sound of wood cracking, which was rather loud. Ludicra turned to see Rollo grasp the clump of treasure because his weight was breaking the limb. Already weakened by the earth-quakes, the tree made a deafening crack behind Ludicra's perch. She, Rollo, and the clump of treasure all plummeted to the bottom of the Great Chasm!

FIFTEEN

Visions Old and New

Now is a good time to fly again! thought Rollo as he plunged headfirst into the gorge. *And Ludicra! She's falling too!*

With every hair on his pelt he willed himself to stop dropping and go up – not for his own sake, but for his beloved's. When he smacked into Ludicra as she fell behind him, he knew it was working.

With a loud grunt Ludicra stopped falling and dangled at the end of a rope. Rollo could see their comrades on the ledge, trying to hold up the heavy troll. Gnat had already fallen off the ledge and was gripping the rope, and Weevil and Crawfleece were about to fall off.

A terrible crash echoed in the canyon as the treasure nest smashed on the rocks below. Half of the baubles bounced into the pool and half into the lava.

Rollo paid no attention as he flew up to the ledge. First he grabbed Gnat by the foot and rescued him, then he steadied Crawfleece and pushed all of them against the cliff. Then the troll landed and grabbed the rope, helping Weevil steady Ludicra.

'Pull her up!' shouted Rollo. When everyone on the ledge had staggered to their feet and begun to haul, they were able to lift Crawfleece a few feet.

Rollo glanced down and saw the stunned elves staring at the scattered treasure as if all the objects were cursed.

'Take it!' shouted Ludicra, shaking her fist at the fey folk. 'Go ahead, Dwayne! You wanted the loot so badly – take it!'

'Ludicra, be still!' ordered Rollo. 'We're trying to rescue you.'

'You'll have to rescue that putrid elf instead!' shouted his princess. 'If I ever get my claws on him!'

As they hauled Ludicra back to the ledge, Crawfleece slapped her brother on the back. 'Good to see you! Leave it to you to bring a dragon to our rescue.'

'Yeah, great job, Rollo!' echoed Weevil. 'You always make a dramatic entrance.'

But the young troll wasn't listening to them, not while Ludicra was still in danger. When they finally dragged her bulky form to safety, he hugged her fiercely.

Ludicra hugged him back and said tearfully, 'Good to see you, too, Rollo. If you ever leave me again, *you'll* need rescuing!'

'I know,' he said hoarsely, with a lump in his throat. He rested his head on the fur of her shoulder and felt as if he were finally home.

Somewhere in the distance a great cheer went up –
it sounded like thousands of voices. Rollo and his
companions looked down to see a mass of trolls gathering on the far side of the lava river. There were trolls
as far as they could see into the distance.

'Rollo! Rollo!' they began to shout. 'Long live the
Troll King! Long live the Troll King!'

'Where did *they* come from?' asked the stunned leader.

'Your friend Filbum arranged them,' said a cheerful
voice just above Rollo's ear.

He cringed when he saw that it was Clipper, but
Ludicra laughed and gripped his arm. 'It's okay –
Clipper turned good again after the serpent knife was
destroyed.'

'Stygius Rex, too,' said the fairy urgently. 'We've got
to find him. A lightning bolt hit him, and he was dashed
onto the rocks.' The fairy darted toward the bottom,
where the elves were gathering to view the aftermath.

Weevil began to lower the rope, and the ogre said,
'Let's be careful going down.'

'Filbum!'

'Crawfleece!'

The happy pair rushed toward each other, and
Crawfleece grabbed the smaller troll, lifted him off the
ground, and spun him around. All the time, Filbum
laughed hysterically.

Rollo was arm-in-arm with Ludicra, and he gazed at
Crawfleece and smiled. A month ago Crawfleece and
Filbum would have been a very unlikely pair – although
no more unlikely than he and Ludicra.

Finally it was Rollo's turn to reunite with his old friend. He wanted to hear Filbum's story of going through the portal, but there were more urgent matters at the moment. The elven leader, Dwayne, walked slowly toward him. His usually pale face was smudged black, and half of his flaxen hair had been burned off. 'There's an army of trolls on the other side of the river,' he said. 'I'm outnumbered by about a thousand to one.'

'It doesn't matter, because there's no more fighting,' said Rollo with a weary sigh. 'This is your side of the chasm, and we're going home. Take the treasure – I have everything I want.' He gripped Ludicra tightly, and she nuzzled his fur.

'There are some wounded ogres and a mage over there.' Dwayne pointed toward a crater where three elves were standing guard.

Weevil led the way, and they all gasped when they saw how burned Captain Chomp, Sergeant Skull, and Gouge were. Stygius Rex was badly hurt from his fall, and he looked as gaunt as a ghoul lying in the reddish glow of the lava.

'They can't be moved,' said Ludicra with concern. 'They need healing.'

'Absolutely right,' answered Dwayne. 'We'll set up a camp here, and we won't move them. But I'm not sure how much our healers can do for them . . . in their condition.'

Suddenly the dark skies of the chasm lit up as if a thousand lanterns were slowly descending. Everyone on both sides of the river gasped in awe as a mass of fairies floated slowly down to the bottom. Leading this ghostly parade was Clipper, and Rollo waved to his friend.

The shimmering fairies alighted gently upon Chomp, Skull, Gouge, Stygius Rex, and everybody else who had been wounded in the struggle. The fairies took the pain and suffering onto themselves, and many had to be cared for afterward. No one paid any attention to the treasure, which lay strewn about like so many dead leaves.

'Rollo! Rollo!' shouted the crowd with joy. 'Long live the Troll King!'

Lights twinkled in the gayly decorated Dismal Swamp, and streamers waved from the top of every standard. The bridges were freshly painted and repaired, and they were full of happy trolls, ogres, gnomes, fairies, and elves. All of Bonespittle was in attendance, and most of the Bonny Woods, too. All were dressed in their finest finery to witness the coronation of the new Troll King.

Atop Rollo's old hovel a large platform had been constructed. Upon this platform the dignitaries were gathered. From Bonespittle: Rollo and Ludicra, of course; Crawfleece, Filbum, Nulneck, Krunkle, Vulgalia, Captain Chomp, Weevil, Runt, Gnat, Sergeant Skull, and Stygius Rex. From the Bonny Woods: Melinda the Enchantress Mother, Prince Dwayne, Prince Thatch, Clipper, the Council of Elves, a host of fairies, and a flock of birds.

A string of well-wishers stretched from the Dismal Swamp to the Forbidden Forest, where the weddings would take place. It was enough to bring tears to an old sorcerer's eyes, and Stygius Rex wept openly.

'Get control of yourself, Master,' whispered Runt, the gnome who used to be the sorcerer's scribe. Beside him stood his proud nephew, Gnat, who wore his new medals of bravery.

'I-I can't help myself!' wailed Stygius Rex with great sobs. 'This is what I saw in my vision, when you came to my chambers that one morning. Do you remember? All of Bonespittle united with joy as they crowned a new king.'

The elder scribe shook his head in amazement. 'Yes, you saw it just like this. Of course, you thought it was *you* being crowned.'

Stygius Rex sniffed back his tears. 'I'm a silly old heap.'

The gnome cocked a hairy eyebrow. 'Didn't you envision a bridge across the Great Chasm?'

'Yes, and that is happening!' said the old mage with excitement. 'Already we have a rope bridge, and Master Krunkle is assembling the crews and lumber to build a *real* bridge. With the help of the fairies, it should go smoothly. When citizens of Bonespittle and the Bonny Woods can walk peacefully between the two lands, then everything in my vision will have come to pass!'

As the crowd cheered the Enchantress Mother walked across the platform to the place where Rollo waited nervously. Melinda looked resplendent in her shimmering white gown, and the elves applauded proudly. Clipper flew beside her, clutching a simple silver crown in her delicate arms. There were dozens of dazzling, jewel-encrusted crowns in the treasure, but Rollo had chosen the simplest one.

'Stygius?' whispered Runt. 'You aren't upset that the Enchantress Mother is conducting this ceremony?'

'No, no!' said the sorcerer, sniffing back tears. 'I am to marry the happy couples in the Forbidden Forest. That was my choice. Ssshh, they're starting.'

The Enchantress Mother was beaming as she gazed at Rollo, and a hush fell over the vast crowd. 'To be here on this special night,' she began, 'is the greatest honor of my life. All of us will brag about how we were here tonight and how we witnessed history in the making. Until Rollo and his companions crossed the Great Chasm, we were ignorant of each other. We harbored hatred, prejudice, and fear about each other.'

Her smile grew broader. 'But one young troll learned that he could stand up for fairness, and he could smash prejudice and hatred. He taught his fellow trolls that they were of noble blood, and he taught longtime enemies that they had nothing to fear. In all of this he was guided by his loyal companions – and his beloved, Ludicra.'

Stygius Rex sobbed loudly, and Runt looked around with embarrassment. Beside him, Gnat tried not to laugh.

Melinda motioned to her fellow elves. 'In time we fey folk learned not to hate Rollo, and we became his companions too. Most importantly we came to know that we were in the presence of greatness. So I am proud to be here to declare Rollo, son of Nulneck and Vulgalia, the newest monarch in a proud line of leaders – the Troll King!'

The cheers that echoed through the Dismal Swamp were deafening. Hats, streamers, and noisemakers were thrown into the sky, and elves and ogres hugged one another with joy. From somewhere in the distance came a gigantic burp that shook the ground and drowned out the cries of delight.

'Old Belch gives his approval!' shouted Captain Chomp, who was still leaning on a crutch. Everyone shared a raucous laugh, even Sergeant Skull, who had a new metal bowl sewn onto his head.

'To the forest to be married!' shouted Crawfleece. The grinning troll grabbed Filbum's hand and dragged him off the platform and down the bridge. When the little troll didn't move fast enough, she picked him up and carried him. The crowd cheered with delight.

Laughing gayly, Ludicra took Rollo's hand and led him onto the bridge. Elves threw beautiful yellow flowers in the path of the portly bride and the new king. The trolls threw dried grubs. Everyone was feasting, and the smell of delicious food overwhelmed the usual swamp stench.

'Come!' said Stygius Rex, grabbing Runt's hand. 'We must be there first!'

With that, the gnome was hauled rudely off the ground by the flying sorcerer, and they sailed over the crowd of merrymakers. Runt screamed in fear, but he told himself that his master was more powerful than ever, now that he was noble.

Soon they landed in the Forbidden Forest, upon another platform, built near a vast, slimy pit. The Hole was filled with the vilest water and meanest snappers and sucker fish in all of Bonespittle. It was the perfect place for a wedding!

It took a while, but the wedding party finally arrived. Ludicra and Rollo were dressed in the finest elven silk, and Crawfleece and Filbum wore troll garb. Both of the female trolls wept with joy and waved to their friends as they waited, while the males grinned dumbly.

Stygius Rex had changed out of his usual somber black and now wore a light blue robe of elven silk. *It's hard to imagine a happier sorcerer*, thought Runt. The warty elder stood beaming at the trolls, and he motioned for the cheering crowd to be quiet.

'Welcome to the Forbidden Forest, one and all!' announced Stygius Rex. 'Not only do we have a new king, but we also have two new hovel mates to celebrate! We come here to bond these two pairs of lovers, but they were already bonded by fire in the Great Chasm. If anyone has proven they deserve to be with each other, it is Ludicra and Rollo. The same for Crawfleece and Filbum.'

The mage's eyes glistened with tears, but he went on. 'They have been loyal and true to each other during difficult trials. They have proven their love time and time again, even when they didn't know they were in love. All of us have been privileged to watch their feelings blossom while they have matured into our leaders. I know they will make each other as happy as they have made all of us.'

Grinning ear to ear, Stygius Rex raised his hands. 'Join me now in greeting our newest hovel mates:

Ludicra and Rollo. Crawfleece and Filbum. You may kiss your troll!'

Both couples embraced, while the crowd cheered insanely. As soon as her kiss ended, Crawfleece grabbed a vine and went sailing over the Hole. She laughed as the snappers' jaws missed her, while Filbum chewed his talons nervously.

Elven musicians began to play a sprightly tune, and everyone at the wedding danced. Clipper and Weevil performed a jig, Rollo danced with Dwayne, and Sergeant Skull danced with the Enchantress Mother. Overhead flew the great momma dragon and her brood of small dragons, and their wings were festooned with colorful streamers.

Long into the night elves and ogres toasted one another, and everyone celebrated the peaceful reign of the Troll King.